THE SEEP

THE SEEP

CHANA PORTER

Excerpt from "My Play" in *Sherwood Forest* by Camille Roy.
Copyright © 2011 by Camille Roy. Reprinted with the
permission of The Permissions Company, LLC on behalf of
Futurepoem Books, www.futurepoem.com. All rights reserved.

Excerpt from *Architectural Body* by Madeline Gins and
Arakawa. Copyright © 2002 by Madeline Gins and Shusaku
Arakawa. Reprinted by permission of The University of
Alabama Press. All rights reserved.

Excerpt from "You are not dead" in *Black Life* by
Dorothea Lasky. Copyright © 2010 by Dorothea Lasky.
Reprinted with the permission of Wave Books, wavepoetry.com.
All rights reserved.

First published by Soho Press
227 W 17th Street
New York, NY 10011

All rights reserved.

Library of Congress Cataloging-in-Publication Data

Porter, Chana, author.
The seep / Chana Porter.

ISBN 978-1-64129-215-3
eISBN 978-1-64129-087-6

1. Science fiction.
PS3616.O766 S44 2020 (print) PS3616.O766 (ebook)
813'.6—dc23

Printed in the United States of America

10 9 8 7 6 5 4 3

My first novel is dedicated to all of the secret writers in my family, particularly to my grandmother Virginia Porter

and

to the magnificent teens of the Octavia Project who show me visions of a better reality through their creative fire

Once people realize that the human race has not yet availed itself of its greatest tool for learning how not to die, they will cease being defeatists in the matter.

—Madeline Gins and Arakawa, *Architectural Body*

———

I would love you if you were dead
but you are not dead you are alive

—Dorothea Lasky, "You Are Not Dead"

———

This is our science story, which I place
in the safe deposit box of your butch heart.

—Camille Roy, "My Play"

THE SEEP

Tips for Throwing a Dinner Party
at the End of the World

RELAX. PEOPLE MAY think they want to indulge,
get too drunk, incapacitate themselves with weed, but
really they just want to appreciate this fragile moment
while the outside world falls down. Your party should
facilitate this easeful enjoyment, not lead loved ones
to panic through overconsumption. Be present. And
remember, you don't know what's happening in the
morning, so while an orgy might very well be the perfect thing, you don't want to spend your last night on
Earth trying to cajole your friends into a particular
kind of revelry. Be present. Clean your apartment until
it sparkles. Shower, of course, and anoint your body
with fragrant oils, but then wear your most beloved
sweatpants. Make a wide selection of delicious food,
high in protein, complex carbohydrates, and healthy

fats. Serve wine but also a lovely selection of herbal teas. Juice spritzers, in fancy goblets, will allow your guests to hydrate while feeling opulent. Remember, if someone starts crying, don't try to shut them down or change the subject. *Be present.* Eventually, the conversation will flow to other things—typically, to The Past and How Great It Was, Even Though We Didn't Know It at the Time, and The Future, that shimmering, mercurial beast, constantly breaking our hearts.

PART ONE
THE SOFTEST
INVASION

I.

When the aliens first made contact, Trina and her not-yet-wife, Deeba, threw one of their famous dinner parties for a select group of friends. It wasn't difficult to keep the guest list small. Everyone was too nervous to travel far, the subways and buses deserted but for the most intrepid or desperate travelers. They invited two beloved couples who happened to live close by, and who wondrously had never met. Emma and Mariam came first, with two types of hard cheeses, three types of olives, gluten-free rice crackers, tubs of spicy hummus. Emma was French and Mariam was from Cairo, so they both really knew how to put together a cheese plate. Their little party was completed by Katharine and Laura, the friendly, easygoing lesbians from Tennessee. They came with copious amounts of alcohol (one can always depend on the lapsed Christians to bring the bar): pale ale for the butches, and drinkable red wine. Introductions were made, drinks were poured, cheese and olives exclaimed over. After a half hour of breezy conversation, Deeba brought out a tureen of her famous fish stew, finished with black pepper and a squeeze of lime. Trina passed around homemade loaves of bread, her one party trick. It was so easy to make, and yet everyone thought she was a magician for adding yeast to water to flour and waiting. The women sopped fragrant soup with crusty bread. A generous feeling swirled around them like a melody, like a scent. The essence of a perfect dinner party. *How have we never met before?* they asked again and again, but what they were really saying was, *How have I only just begun to love you?*

Throwing a dinner party was all Trina and Deeba could think to do. They had already filled the bathtub with clean water and made sure all of their flashlights had new batteries. They kept checking their most reliable sources on Twitter, as well as Al Jazeera, *The New York Times*, *The Guardian*. Every source said to keep calm, try not to panic, and to stop it with these suicide pacts. *Unbelievable*, the newscasters kept saying, *it's unbelievable*. That word had been ringing in Trina's head all day. But what was believable about this world, about her government, about what they were doing to the planet and each other? Furthermore, what did Trina believe in with total certainty? That the sun rose in the morning? That the sky was blue? These aliens could say that the cosmos was being carried on the back of a great platypus and she'd have to believe them. What was more mutable than her own perceptions? Katharine raised her wineglass. Her toast became the answer to Trina's unspoken questions. At the time, Trina thought this was a coincidence.

Katharine spoke warmly, as if she were telling a long joke. "Lately," she said, "I've felt as if I've been living in the wrong timeline. I've become numb, like I'm watching my own life as a movie, that is, when I'm not filled with rage or tremendous grief or crippling depression."

Deeba hooted and cheered. Emma's brown eyes twinkled in the candlelight. "Every day, I wake up embarrassed by my country and what we've become—"

"Ugh," groaned Mariam. She took on the tone of a newscaster. "Now, more than ever . . . In these trying times . . ." Trina laughed and slapped the table.

"Let her finish!" chided Deeba.

Katharine cleared her throat. "As I was saying! I'm embarrassed by what we've become, and by what we always have been and have never addressed."

"Hear, hear," said Emma, raising her glass.

"But tonight," Katharine continued. "Looking at your beautiful faces, I can finally, safely say that I have no idea what's coming! I don't know if this is the end of life as we know it, or the beginning of a grand adventure, or perhaps both. All I have is my uncertainty. And really, that's all I've ever had. Everything else was a lie." She took a long swallow from her glass. "So cheers, babes. To tonight." The women clapped and toasted, whistling. Katharine took a half bow and sat down. Laura slung an arm around her wife and grinned. Trina looked across the table at Deeba's round, brown face. Her cheeks were warm with wine, as pink as the inside of a rose. *I know that I love you*, thought Trina. *And that's enough for me.* From across the table, Deeba winked.

AFTER DINNER, THE women lounged on the floor and got a bit stoned. And then someone decided it would be fun to take a bath. They would soon realize that The Seep had already infiltrated their city's water supply. They were already compromised, already bodily hosts to their new alien friends. It was through that connection they could hear one another's thoughts, feel the same emotions, overlaid with the all-consuming adage that Everything Will Be All Right, No Matter What. The softest invasion had begun.

2.

Eventually, everyone understood that those who had already made contact with the aliens felt fine about the extraterrestrial invasion, while those who had not felt no shortage of panic, despair, rage, and powerlessness. There was talk of launching a war, but on what? Those who had been touched by the alien presence simply felt no fear. When connected with the aliens through water or bodily fluids, it was impossible to feel anything except expansive joy, peace, tenderness, and love. But were humans still human without their worries? Or were the aliens placating them with these good feelings for some other, darker purpose?

The answer was—as these things so often are—all of the above. It's never how we want it, clear-cut and shining, a perfect moral center leading us all back home. The Seep did love us, and it wanted to help us to create a perfect world. And this destroyed life as we knew it.

AT FIRST, TRINA cherished the invasion, the casual overthrow of everything that had felt codified but broken for so long. In the past, she had rejected the concept that the world was becoming kinder. There had always been scapegoats and underclasses, no matter if they were locked away in prisons or working in factories in other countries. And on top of that, she was broke! She was in a fair amount of debt and her apartment was near a Superfund site, yet she felt grateful to be close to the subway. Her multiple jobs didn't pay her enough, she was stressed-out and tired all the time, her artwork was suffering, and the government couldn't decide if they wanted to take away her healthcare. The aliens changed all of that. You could hold a product in your hand and feel its history, feel people's attitudes and emotions as they'd processed the materials. Struggles that had felt impossibly uphill were now suddenly so clear, as if everyone had awoken one morning from the same dream. It was insanity to poison your environment to save a dime. It was insanity to build bigger and bigger bombs to keep the peace. Guns were melted down into scrap metal. Police officers put their uniforms away.

Trina's inner and outer worlds expanded and merged. Her city became a tangled nest of permaculture, no separation between living, growing, making—a forest, a garden, a farm next to a coffee shop, a museum, a hospital, a school. All debts were forgiven. The student-loan people threw away their phones. After years of struggle in the old scarcity paradigm, Trina finally had freedom to think about what she wanted to do with her copious time. That first year, she didn't do much of anything. She, like most people, was just really high on The Seep, watching her own miraculous hands as they moved, touching her wooden coffee table to connect to the essence of the tree it had once been (pretty boring to watch, but pretty fun to experience). She spent one full summer understanding her body as a convenient container for her immortal essence.

Deeba was first to shake off their hazy elastic stupor. She went back into her film work, finally shooting her first feature. This got Trina out of her daze. She returned to painting. Eventually, her work was shown in galleries and museums around the world. And because art was no longer a commodity (nothing was), some lucky people had Trina's paintings in their homes. Deeba started making documentaries about The Seep's new emergent subcultures—the yellow-meeks, the decomposers/living dead, pain cults, pearl houses, that kind of thing. Trina moved into performance, both sound and video, involving her own body in the practice. She got a little bit famous and had some minor love affairs, made Deeba proud of her celebrity wife. Then she got bored of the art world; of its pageantry, its emphasis on personality. Trina went back to school and became a doctor. How proud her mother would have been! (Too bad she killed herself when the aliens came.) Trina and Deeba lived and thrived, grew and changed, amongst their constantly shifting, abundant world, for years and years. Until one day, when Deeba looked at Trina from across the breakfast nook and said she wanted to become a child again.

THE NIGHT BEFORE, they had been at a full-moon party in Bernal Heights. Among the guests were their old friends Emma and Mariam; Peaton and Allie, therapists who were both heavy into Seep meditation practices; and the musician Horizon Line, a rather famous Seep artist with whom Trina used to tour during her brief stint as a rock-and-roller. Emma was showing off her newest Seep modifications, her scratchy cat tongue and retractable claws, licking the neck of anyone who volunteered. Mariam was seriously considering getting hooves, which she explained were excellent for rock climbing, making devilish jokes at sex parties, and, apparently, relieving pressure from your knees. When Deeba said casually that she might want to be parented again, Trina thought she was joking.

"I saw a video of someone turning into a baby," Deeba said. "It was on someone's transformations channel on the Electric Spirit. You know, there are people who are busy becoming everything, and recording it all for us to watch."

Trina shuddered. "To think, we've lived long enough to be in a future where everyone is a fucking performance artist." She drank a little off the top of her punch glass and frowned. The front taste was Cara Cara orange juice, made fizzy with carbonation, cut through with something acidic and bright like lemongrass. But the unmistakable metallic tinge of The Seep was there at the end, an oily sensation that snaked down her throat like blood. "Say what you want about the old days," she said, pushing the glass away. "The art was better then."

Allie looked like she was about to cry, as she had lately when anyone said anything remotely controversial. "You can't be serious, Trina. You're not actually one of those people who believe you need suffering to make great art!"

Trina shook her head. "I'm not, I swear. But I do think there's a lack of rigor at the present moment. And these kids, you know, these Children of the Seep—they seem so unmotivated, so disorganized. They hardly get anything done!"

"These kids today!" joked Mariam, wagging her fingers.

Horizon, however, nodded. "Trina, I completely agree. Things were different when we all thought we were going to die, when we had no knowledge of our immortal souls, so focused on these temporary containers." He sipped deeply from his punch. "But of *course* the things we made were different when we thought we were mortal. How could they not be?"

"Right, but I don't think it's terrible to say that a little bit of hardship, a little tension, makes for more interesting art." Trina looked around the table. "When was the last time you saw something that really moved you?"

Peaton made a sweeping gesture with his punch glass. "I experience moving works of creation all the time!"

"But are you high on The Seep when you're experiencing the art?"

Peaton shrugged. "Well, of course."

Trina leaned back from the table. "My point exactly. We don't make things that can stand on their own anymore."

At her side, Deeba giggled. "Hey, Trina, the Compound called. They want you to interrogate your scarcity mentality."

Trina laughed and gave her wife's round thigh a squeeze.

"Ouch, Deeba!" said Peaton. "That's not a very nice thing to say."

Allie touched Trina's hand from across the table. "Do you want to pause and process your emotions? We can go into the other room."

Trina resisted the urge to roll her eyes. When had everyone stopped having a sense of humor? "No, no, it's a joke—an inside joke. We've been saying it for years." She looked around at her oldest friends. Their faces suddenly seemed horribly alien with all their Seep modifications: Allie's angel wings, Peaton's bejeweled forehead, Emma's cat tongue. Even Horizon, who looked exactly the same as he had when they were on tour together all those years ago, looked eerie because he had not changed at all. Not a single wrinkle around his dark eyes or crease next to his full mouth. His smooth, tan skin was flawless, unmarked by time, the face of an eternally young man. Even his hairstyle was exactly the same, the long, dark hair reaching down to his waist like a curtain.

"Hey, the Compound called," said Deeba in a silly, high-pitched voice. She sipped more punch. "Which is funny in itself, since no one uses phones anymore!"

"The Compound called," growled Trina like a monster. Deeba shrieked with laughter. Peaton relaxed, but Allie was still frowning, her eyes big and wet. Trina went on. "They want you to come live with them, Trina, because you're a buzzkill, an old fuddy-duddy, a has-been. The Compound called, and they think you should just give up!"

Everyone laughed. Even Allie smiled a little. Trina stood up from the table. She went into the kitchen to find some wine. No more weird punch, thank you. She poured a glass at the counter, her bare feet sinking pleasantly into the squishy, moss-covered floor. She found most New Order–style houses a bit tacky, like something from a low-budget B movie about a pleasure planet, but Peaton and Allie had good taste. She watched bright schools of fish swim to and fro in the floor-to-ceiling aquarium wall, sizing up her own reflection in the glass. Old Levi's, hoodie, ancient leather boots. *Hey, the Compound called to say they like your outfit,* Deeba liked to say, hooking her finger through a belt loop of Trina's worn jeans. Nowadays, everyone wore gossamer hoods and collars of lace, feathers and leaves sewn into elaborate dresses. That could never be Trina's style. What was a diesel butch to do?

She sipped her wine. *The Compound called . . .* she thought, *and they want their phone back.* When The Seep had first come, the idea of joining the Compound had been laughable to Trina. How insulting, how repugnant, that some faction had decided the status quo was worth protecting.

But maybe there was a kernel of truth buried under all of Deeba's good-natured barbs. *The Compound called . . .* Lately, everything Trina could think to say was a complaint. That art wasn't good anymore, performance or otherwise. That most new music was meant to be listened to on The Seep, which made for an amazing experience, sure, but how could you accurately judge the artistry if you were high? No one Trina asked could answer that question. Like Peaton, they didn't seem to understand why she would ask it at all. No one read books or watched the great cinema of days gone by. Trina and Deeba had met at a Derek Jarman screening so many moons ago. Jarman would have liked the aliens. But would he have continued making films? Or would he just have enjoyed life, tended to his garden, and lived out his days happy and healthy? And if so, was that so bad? Trina didn't make art anymore; she was a doctor. It wasn't a betrayal of her old self to change. And yet these questions kept her up at night in her mostly happy bed with Deeba, little thorns in her side.

Still, for the first many years of living with The Seep, joy was all around her, like a cloud, a mist. From the kitchen, she could hear Mariam telling a long joke in what sounded like Arabic. Everyone laughed. Emma started singing a folk song in French.

Trina poured a little more wine into her glass

and stayed, watching the fish swim lazily across the long wall of water. And all the emotional processing! It wasn't just Allie and Peaton, either. Nowadays everyone expected you to talk about your feelings all day long. Not just lovers or close friends, either. Joe Shmoe on the street wanted to show you his dream journal. Trina had learned long ago (through the patience of a very loving Deeba) to open up about her feelings, her childhood, all that ancient history. But now, it seemed like everyone wanted to share their innermost emotions as casually as if asking for the time. At her last volunteer shift at the food co-op, Trina had spent two hours processing a random woman's latest past-life regression while shelving cans of chickpeas. It was too much.

TRINA READIED HERSELF and went back to the dining room. The party had moved to the living room floor. Everyone was trading foot massages, reclined on colorful pillows, the punch bowl in the center of the room.

"We're doing a toasting ritual, Trina!" called Peaton. "What do you want to toast to?" He poured from the punch bowl and held the glass out to her.

Trina gestured with her wineglass. "I'm good, thank you."

"It's better if you drink the same thing as us, Trina," said Allie earnestly. "Better for the ritual to be a cohesive unit."

Trina suppressed an eye roll. She accepted the glass but set it down next to her. Sometimes it was better to agree than argue. Deeba wriggled her little brown feet into her lap. Trina smiled and started rubbing her wife's fat lovely toes.

Mariam raised her glass high. "Let's toast to Trina, for becoming a doctor!" Everyone raised their glasses of punch. "It's nice to be useful, isn't it, old girl?"

Trina grinned. "You know, it really is."

"To being useful!" shouted Horizon Line. "And, as I have remained a humble artist, to being unuseful! And apparently, not as good as I used to be." He cackled. Everyone toasted anew. Trina hit Horizon lightly on the thigh. He winked a pretty eye at her.

"I think you mean useless," said Emma, taking out her claws.

Trina turned to Deeba. "Is this punch Seeped?"

"Darling, it's a party," Deeba murmured. "And we're not working tomorrow. Don't worry about it."

"I should know what I'm putting in my body." Trina raised her voice. "Sorry—Peaton? Allie? Dinner was amazing, by the way. Is this punch Seeped? I have a long day tomorrow at the clinic." She saw Deeba's mouth twitch at the lie. Whatever.

Peaton considered. "Very lightly Seeped," he said slowly. "I don't even feel it."

Trina snorted. Peaton communed with The Seep for hours in meditation every day; of course he didn't feel it. "Well, you know I'm a lightweight."

"I'll get you a charcoal water," said Allie, pushing up to her feet. "I'm sorry, that was thoughtless of us." She looked like she was about to cry again. "I just wanted all of us to be on the same page, you know?" She frowned at Trina's wineglass. "Alcohol has a really challenging energy for me right now."

Trina grimaced. "Uh, sorry?" But Allie had already gone into the kitchen.

"You know," said Mariam, "I read that charcoal water is a total placebo. It doesn't actually flush out The Seep from your system."

Emma tilted her head. "It works for me, I've used it lots of times."

"Well," said Deeba. "Placebos work, at least some of the time. Belief is important." Allie came back with the charcoal water and placed it in front of Trina.

Trina opened it and drank. "Thank you."

"Oh, no, babe," said Emma. "You broke Trina's placebo!" She laughed. "Right? If she doesn't believe in it, it won't work."

"I think the real question is, why is Trina so hesitant about joining with The Seep?" asked Peaton. "They are our greatest teachers. We can learn so much from them." His eyes swirled with the telltale blue-green of alien intervention. "Just think about our poor friends in the Compound, cut off from it all."

Trina snorted. "You can learn things from books, too. Not like anyone reads anymore."

"Yes, that's exactly my point," said Peaton. "Why would you passively read a book, when you can join with The Seep and experience the world on the most visceral and connected level?"

"What I want to know is how the kids in the Compound feel about all of this," said Emma. "I mean, their parents choose to live separately from the alien influence, and that's their prerogative, but do their children have a choice? I know we're all free to do as we wish, but sometimes being free to do something affects those in your care. It's not right!"

Deeba's mouth folded into a little line, which meant she was thinking hard. "I think you have to do what you think is right, no matter what. And of course that affects the people you love, but you still have to do what you know is best."

"Trina, do you agree?" asked Peaton.

"I do agree, my baby is so smart." Trina kissed Deeba's foot. "But I'm trying to get laid tonight, so I have ulterior motives." Deeba laughed her wonderful, throaty laugh. Peaton and Allie exchanged glances.

"Think of the children!" shouted Mariam. "Won't someone think of the poor Compound children?" She raised her glass up for another toast. Trina suppressed a yawn. She discreetly glanced at her watch, but Deeba caught the gesture.

"Hey, lover, the Compound called," she whispered. "They want their watch back." Trina could see the tinge of The Seep in her wife's eyes. She was high. They wouldn't be leaving this party anytime soon. Trina wanted to go home, eat ice cream, have sex, and then watch old episodes of *Star Trek: Deep Space Nine* on the Electric Spirit. It was looking like none of those things would happen now.

"Hey, Trina," said Horizon, putting down his punch. "Wanna get some air?"

"Oh, no, Horizon," said Allie, her eyes filling with tears. "Are you still smoking? It's so bad for you!"

Trina smiled at her old friend. He could read her like a freaking book. "You know, I really do."

"Maybe for my next performance piece I'll grow new lungs," said Horizon, winking at Allie. He and Trina pulled on their shoes and wandered off toward the back garden.

3.

"That's better," said Horizon Line. They stood in the garden and looked up at the sky. Next to the bench was a little stone sculpture of an angel covering her face. The moon was full and bright. "I fear I have lost my taste for crowds."

"I almost forgot this was a full-moon party," said Trina. Everything was vaguely Wiccan nowadays, lots of tracking of the moon cycles and nature worship, but without all that deity stuff. Trina liked the emphasis on ritual, and how you could approach spirituality as a choose-your-own-adventure. Religion was low-stress and low-maintenance, just like everything else. She tugged on Horizon's glossy black hair. "Hey, thanks for saving me back there. Do you think Peaton's going to push for an orgy?" She thought back to Deeba's plump little feet in her lap, her smiling round face, drunk on The Seep. It wasn't as nice as her own bed with ice cream to follow, but Trina could get in the mood to fool around a little in the company of old friends. Especially if it would stop all that circular, boring Seep talk. Conversing with high people was not how she wanted to spend a Saturday night.

Hey, Trina, the Compound called, and they want their paradigm back.

She gazed up at the bright full moon. Suddenly, the old joke stung a bit. Maybe she really was living in the past.

Horizon shook his head. "No orgy tonight, my sweet. Word on the street is that he and Allie have both taken vows of celibacy."

Trina nearly spit out her charcoal water. "Are you serious?"

"Yeah, but don't ask them about it or they'll never shut up. Apparently, they're directing all of their 'lower energies' into their Seep meditations, having orgasms that last three hours, seeing God, that kind of stuff."

"Huh," said Trina. About fifteen years ago, Allie had spent a weekend tied to her and Deeba's four-poster bed. Trina had forgotten how fun that had been. Allie used to be fun too, and sharply weird, a little neurotic in a way that felt totally rational. Now everything made her spacey and weepy. It couldn't be good for your emotional health to have transcendental experiences every single day. No wonder Allie was coming apart at the seams. "Celibacy, eh?" Trina sighed. "The world will never stop surprising me." She took a cigarette from Horizon and lit up. She inhaled and choked. "What is this?"

He laughed. "It's just sage and raspberry leaf. Allie's right, I can't do tobacco anymore. When I'm Seeped, I can literally feel my cells dying. It sucks!"

"Well, then don't Seep so much. Come over to my

side." She deeply wished it was a real cigarette, and that she hadn't left her wineglass inside.

Horizon looked up at the sky, the angles of his face accented by moonlight. "I do wonder if we're using The Seep in the best way we can." He took a long drag. "I mean, we've been given this amazing gift, and we're using it to, what, grow unicorn horns? There has to be more."

Trina considered this. "I hear you, man, I really do. But the work we do with it at the hospital is beautiful. There's so much happening—probably a lot of Seep tech we don't even know about." Just yesterday Trina had used The Seep to erase a tumor from a woman's breast. No cutting, no incision, no radiation or chemotherapy, just the power of Seep consciousness speaking into this woman's cells, telling them how to die gracefully, to let go and become something new. The procedure took twenty minutes, and then the woman went to a hula-hoop meet-up in Golden Gate Park. There were ways to use The Seep that were productive and healthy and didn't make you high for hours on end. One just had to be a little thoughtful.

"Yes, yes, yes," Horizon said. "I know The Seep

improves our lives in a million big and small ways. What I mean is that we've gotten lazy. We're using the things we used to care about as a rubric for success."

Trina smiled. "Well, old friend, you could use The Seep for something other than keeping your wrinkles at bay." She brushed his smooth cheek with her fingertip. "Or shall I call you Dorian?"

He blinked at her. Did she have to explain the reference? "Trina," said Horizon slowly. "I'll tell you a secret. This is something that no one else knows. But you're my oldest and dearest friend, and I want to share this with you." He took a big breath and smiled. "This isn't my real face."

"Excuse me?" Trina had only ever known Horizon looking just this way, for the past twenty years.

"This is the exact replica of my boyfriend, Tomas, who died in 1993. I modified myself to look like him as soon as I realized it was possible." His voice carried a hint of smugness. "I think I might have been the first person to use The Seep in this way. It was rather rudimentary back then. If I were to do it again now, my merger with The Seep would be far more sophisticated. So now you know the secret. This face will never wrinkle or age, because it can't. It's more like a mask than anything else."

Trina rubbed her arms. She felt suddenly cold in the night air. "You took this man's identity? Is that what you're telling me, Horizon?"

He tilted his head. His beautiful face, unmarked by time, now looked ghoulish in the moonlight. "Oh, I'm sure you understand," he said.

"Understand what?"

"I know you never got any Seep mods, but you must have had something done, back in the day. Taken hormones or gotten surgery?" Trina raised her eyebrows. "Never mind, it's none of my business."

"No," she said. "It's not. And it's not the same thing at all." She shook her head. "Horizon—what did you look like before?"

He shrugged. "Like a million other people. You wouldn't have noticed me at all."

Trina's eyes grew big. "Hold up—were you a white guy? And you took this brown kid's face?"

Horizon raised an eyebrow but said nothing.

"You didn't! Horizon!" She looked around, almost expecting there to be hidden cameras in the bushes, as if this were all some retro prank. "You can't—you can't take other people's faces, their races, and wear them like—like a suit!"

"Oh, race is a construction," he said, waving his hand. "Everyone knows that."

"That might be, but it's still meaningful. Constructs mean things."

Horizon grew impatient. "Trina, everyone who has been joined even once with The Seep knows that we're all the same. We're all of the same essences, all layers of identity are just that, layers, and you can play with them just as we play with our appearances—"

"Some things are too far. You can't—"

He stood up a little taller, flipping his long black hair over his shoulder. "But I can, Trina. I did. With The Seep, anything is possible. Our bodies are just containers for our immortal essences. And that's my exact point. We've become too narrow in our thinking. Remember how intense it used to be, when you first Seeped? Now we drink punch at a party and barely feel anything!"

"I feel things," she said slowly. "Our bodies may be containers, but they still carry specific histories. And those histories are still meaningful. Of course The Seep doesn't understand that—they're amorphous beings with no physical bodies! But I won't let you stand here, looking like that, and tell me that my history is interchangeable with yours."

He shrugged again. "Well, you can feel however you want about it, obviously."

"Horizon, listen to me. You're being so color-blind it's racist!"

He looked stung, as if she had struck him. "I can't believe you would use that word on me. How long have you known me?"

"Clearly, we don't know each other very well at all. I don't even know what you really look like!"

Horizon threw his cigarette butt to the ground. The grass swallowed it up instantly, taking it back to the earth. "This is what I look like, Trina, and that's my point. Our bodies are completely malleable. We haven't been given this gift to just grow gills, or to sprout angel wings. There has to be something more, something greater to achieve, through The Seep—"

Just then, Deeba's round, shaved head peered out

of the door. "Everything okay out here?" she asked. Then she giggled. "Allie wants to show us pictures of her trip to India. My love, should we call it a night?"

"Yes!" Trina stomped out her cigarette. The ground started sucking up around Trina's shoes. "Hey, watch it!" She wrenched her feet up from the ground.

Horizon breathed deep. "I forgive you, Trina, for calling me that word. I know you didn't mean it."

Trina rubbed her forehead. She was suddenly so tired. "Horizon, I do mean it. If you can't acknowledge that what you're doing is fucked-up, I don't know what to tell you."

His lovely face was blank with surprise. "I have made my whole career as a memorial to my dead lover. What is more thoughtful than that?"

"Well, he didn't get a say in it, did he?" Trina took her wife's hand and turned toward the door.

"You can't judge things based on the way the world was thirty years ago, T. Everything has changed!"

Trina turned back toward him. "You know, I'm going to tell people about you. That they're looking into the face of a dead boy who never gave you his consent. That every person you fuck is fucking the mask of a dead person. How can you not see how creepy, how violent that is?"

Horizon looked at her gravely. "I'll tell people myself, Trina. And when they react with pleasantry, or with boredom, or when they try to show me pictures of their trip to India, you'll see just how mired in the past you are."

She laughed, but the sound was hollow, joyless. "If you're right, I don't think I want to live here anymore. Good night." Trina and Deeba left the garden. They made their apologies to their hosts and walked out into the quiet, lush street.

4.

"Can you believe him?" asked Trina later that evening, lying in bed with Deeba. Their home had very few Seep modifications, but Deeba had insisted their ceiling be a huge roof window open onto the sky. The moonlight was so bright, Trina couldn't see any stars.

"I can," said Deeba. "Peaton and Allie make a big show of how much they Seep, but Horizon is dosed practically all the time. And I agree with you. It's dangerous, all that 'nonseparation, we're all the same, there is no good or bad' stuff. Makes accountability very slippery."

Trina rubbed her eyes. One couldn't really blame The Seep for the inability to make distinctions like race. Before they were joined with life on Earth, they didn't have corporeal forms, a concept of linear time, or even emotions. But that made it so humans needed to be even more thoughtful, more nuanced. "That's exactly why The Seep needs us, maybe more than we need them. And I'm not one of those Keep Earth Human people holed up in the Compound."

Deeba snuggled in close. "Hey, babe," she murmured. "The Compound called. They're sad you don't want to join them."

Trina was too shaken up to laugh. "I really can't believe Horizon would do such a thing and compare it to my transition."

Deeba practically yelled in her ear. "He did *what*?"

"Oh yeah, I didn't even tell you that part." She leaned over and propped up on her elbows. "And then he acted all high and mighty, and tried to *forgive* me! The nerve." In the darkness, Trina could hear Deeba swallow.

"What did you mean when you said, 'I don't want to live here anymore'?"

"Oh, I don't know," said Trina lightly. She gave her wife's soft waist a squeeze and affected a cartoon voice. "Sometimes I think, hey, stop the world, I want to get off." But Deeba didn't laugh. She let Trina's statement hang in the air like fog.

IN THE MORNING, Trina was cooking oatmeal when Deeba brought up the channel on the Electric Spirit, the one with the video of the woman becoming a child, for a second time.

Trina cringed. "Ugh. Why do you want to watch that?"

Deeba pressed her head into Trina's shoulder. "I thought maybe we could watch it together."

Trina turned off the stove and doled out two bowls. "Why would we do that?"

"It doesn't look painful at all, it looks cathartic."

"I don't think it would be painful. Deebs, what are you saying?"

Deeba added dried cherries and chopped walnuts to her oatmeal and stirred. "Ever since I saw that video, I haven't been able to stop thinking about it." A high, airy laugh escaped her throat. "I think I'm losing my mind!"

Trina stood very still. "Oh?"

She looked up at her wife. "Isn't it amazing, Trina? To think about going back to the beginning? All those years of therapy. The old wounds never really heal, do they?" Her eyes were large and strange. "I could do it all over again. With good people this time. Get the parenting I deserve."

Suddenly, Trina was nauseous. She pushed her bowl of oatmeal away. "What are you saying? That you want to die? Now? At forty-six years old?"

"Oh, no sweetheart, no—" She took Trina's hand in hers. "I'm saying I want to live. Without all these memories. Without that old pain. Don't you see the difference?"

Trina spoke very slowly. "Without me, you mean."

"Well," said Deeba carefully, "you would make a very good mother."

Trina's eyes grew wide. "Are you joking, Deeba?

Wait." She grabbed the medicine bag she kept by the door and took out her flashlight. "Are you still high? Let me see your pupils."

"I was afraid of this. I'm not high. Get that thing out of my face."

"Who would understand this? You want me to be your mother? I'm your *wife*!"

Deeba tossed her head. "But we've all been everything to each other—mother, father, lover, sister, brother, endless lifetimes of cycling through roles and reversals."

"That's philosophy, that's spirituality—"

Deeba's face was sad. "That's the truth, Trina, and you know it. Through The Seep."

Trina held up her hands. "Fine. Yes, if you think about it, we've all been everything, but that doesn't mean I'm going to go become an earthworm, does it? Of course not! I'm a human being!"

When Deeba spoke next, her voice was low and serious. "We have a choice about when and how we move on to the next lifetime. That's so amazing! I don't see why you wouldn't want to be connected to me, to love me in a new way. I think it's sort of romantic."

Trina shook her head hard. "I can't believe this. You're talking about leaving me."

"No!" said Deeba sharply. "You're not listening. I'm talking about becoming a child again. And I would do that with you, if you're open to it. You're the one talking about leaving me, Trina. Not the other way around."

TRINA FELT LIKE screaming, felt like ripping out her own hair, like punching a wall, but she just sat on the kitchen floor and cried. She didn't get up for almost a day. For a while, Deeba sat next to her and held her, when Trina would allow herself to be touched. But eventually, Deeba got tired of sitting on the floor. Deeba got up. She came back periodically to ask if Trina wanted tea or anything to eat. In their wedding vows, they had made no promises about forever. It was bad luck to make promises you were unable to keep, and forever was a long time, especially now that death was an opt-in procedure. Trina had imagined they might grow apart in all their years together, or take other lovers who filled them with more passion, or perhaps melt into a kind of friendship, as so many other couples did. But none of those things had happened. Trina loved Deeba now more than ever. She loved her more than on their wedding day. She loved her even more than at that dinner party so many years ago, when she looked across the table and realized that if the sky were to turn green and fish to walk on land, the only thing she needed to make sense about life was being with Deeba. And through The Seep, that wonderful, terrible Seep, Trina knew that Deeba felt that deepest love for her, too. Through The Seep, Deeba understood that Trina would stay with her for another lifetime or maybe more, as wives and roommates, lovers and best friends, through cooking and dinner parties and career shifts, through the boredom and the freedom of unexpected immortality. Through The Seep, Trina knew that Deeba would cherish being connected to Trina for another lifetime or more, but in another role, if only Trina would let her. They could cycle through together endlessly, learning how to love each other in different permutations of being, in something bigger and grander and stranger than pure romance. Love as a verb, an action, an adventure in knowing. But Trina just couldn't hack it. She was old-fashioned that way. Simultaneously, this broke both of their hearts.

ONE NIGHT DURING all of this, Trina dreamt that Deeba was on a floating island, and Trina was on a separate floating island, and it was nighttime. The water around them was very dark. Deeba and Trina looked at each other while they floated slowly yet steadily apart. It was a stupid and obvious dream, and Trina was angry at herself for having it.

TRINA AND DEEBA enacted the same circular argument until it felt like they were actors in a play going through the same performance night after night, their words hollow, their crying choreographed. There was nothing more to say, and they still couldn't see each other's perspective. Neither would bend or budge, and they both felt horribly wronged.

Deeba went to a healer. She made it clear that she did not just want to look like a child; she wanted to actually *be* a child, with a child's sense of wonder and capacity for growth. She wanted to learn how to speak again, perhaps in another language, in a land far away from the wounds of her past. She wanted to dream in another language, to grow a new mother tongue. She would become a perfect little baby. Deeba contacted a party planner who specialized in these kinds of events. The party planner helped her pick a venue, a theme, a motif. Deeba would have her transformation at the beach, near her favorite part of Golden Gate Park. The theme would be the Transformational Nature of Water, with an ice feature and a fog machine. The colorscape would be blue and gold.

"Please don't do this," said Trina on the morning of her wife's transformation. "Please, please, please reconsider." She laughed from pain, a terrible, broken sound. "I'm literally begging you. Stay with me, Deeba. I know you still love me."

Deeba shook her head. "I really thought that you would do this with me." She had found a nice Persian couple living in the South of France. They were very excited to parent her when she was ready. "There's still time to change your mind—"

"Please, not another word. I can't even hear you say it again."

"Listen to yourself! You can't even hear it? How is that remotely helpful?" Deeba's eyes filled with tears. "I don't want to leave you either! Don't you see how sad this makes me?"

Trina made an ugly sound from the back of her throat. "Then don't do it! It's so fucking simple."

Deeba looked at the floor. "Will you come to the ceremony, at least? Will you hold my hand as I move on?" Trina watched as the tears streaked her wife's soft, beautiful face. "I'm scared."

Trina turned away. "Will I go to your funeral, you mean?"

"It isn't like that! You're looking at this all wrong!"

Trina stared at her hands. The thin gold wedding band glinted back at her. "I can't see it any other way. I'm sorry."

Deeba looked at her in disbelief. "I am standing here asking you to love me in every way possible. I am asking you to walk through life with me in whatever form I take. I'm asking you to be my everything, Trina!" She squeezed her hand. "Isn't that worth considering?"

Trina crossed her arms. "You're holding my life hostage."

"That may be so." Deeba brushed the tears away from her face. "You think you'd be happy with another thirty years of watching old movies and eating ice cream with me, but you can't fool me. You aren't happy, Trina. You haven't been happy for a long time."

Trina shrugged. She was too tired to lie. "So?"

Deeba exhaled. "I love you, Trina FastHorse Goldberg-Oneka. Thank you for the sweetest years of my life."

"Please. Please, please don't leave me."

Deeba smiled sadly. "Go figure out who you are without me, babe." She gave her wife a sweet, short kiss. "I hope you find some joy in this weird new world. I really do." And then she left. Trina didn't know if Deeba turned back for one last look. She was too busy crying.

IT FELT AKIN to coming home one day to find that your wife had become a hawk, with dusty talons and a great golden eye. Your hawk-wife can't live with you anymore. She wants to live in the sky and eat smaller birds, not drink coffee and read the newspaper in bed with you. There were tons of stories of these kinds of transformations, and the grief experiences of the loved ones left behind. They flocked to churches built around worshipping the past. Trina never went to church—not before the aliens came, and certainly not after. Instead, she became weirdly obsessed with this gum from what was once Japan. She gathered all of the remaining packages left in the world. When the gum was over, Trina decided, she would find a good way to disappear— death, or whatever came closest to it. Five years after Deeba's passing, Trina only had one twelve-piece package left. She popped one in her mouth and started chewing. She ignored the messages from Peaton and Allie, from Emma and Mariam, from coworkers and former classmates and well-meaning nosy neighbors. She also got an old handgun from some spaced-out magician living in a van on Fish-merman's Wharf. He had called it a "destroyer of worlds," an epithet Trina found corny but secretly thrilling. She liked touching the cold metal. It made her feel in control. With her gun and her gum, Trina decided she didn't need any other kind of company. After Deeba left, Trina forgot her old life and went to the bar instead. She attempted to drown, slowly, from the inside out. These were the things The Seep gave us, and what it took away.

PART TWO
SO, YOUR
TRUE LOVE
HAS BECOME
A BABY

5.

So, Your True Love Has Become a Baby

The Seep is very sorry for your loss. We recognize that you are feeling an incredible amount of pain right now. We want you to know that YOU ARE NOT ALONE, unless, of course, you'd like to be. The Seep cherishes all emotions, even sadness and grief! Just because you're not happy, that doesn't mean you're living life wrong! But if you'd like to feel better sooner, please check the index of your pamphlet to see the different kinds of counseling available to you at this time . . .

TRINA PRESSED THE console next to her bed. A clock appeared, but she couldn't seem to register the time, or whether it was night or day. A small light flashed in the corner of the screen, notifying her that there were messages for her on the Electric Spirit. She ignored them. When was the last time she had eaten? She could starve in bed like this, rehashing the irrevocable past.

Pulling a well-worn bathrobe over her sweatpants, Trina found slippers and slouched over to the kitchen. The water feature in the middle of the floor was slick with algae; the poor fish were probably dead. Trina pulled the sleeve of a shirt out from the water, but as she balled it up, she realized it had been Dee-ba's—a really ratty shirt she wore for gardening. Trina clutched it to her chest. The hollow ache was back. She felt nauseous, light-headed, sick. She needed to eat something. Trina threw the shirt back on the floor.

It landed on a pile of old magazines. She picked up a few dirty dishes as she made her way toward the kitchen. The days-old food crusted around edges of plates and bowls was beginning to stink. She loaded up the sink with soapy water and crammed as many dishes in as she could. She'd wash them after she ate.

TRINA MADE A bowl of oatmeal and sprinkled it with a little cinnamon, congratulating herself on putting in the effort to season the food. She was out of fruit, fresh vegetables, and milk for her tea, but the thought of leaving the house was too much to bear.

Go figure out who you are without me.

Trina pushed the oatmeal away. *Easy for you to say, babe.* Before Deeba, eating was one of those annoying things you had to do because you started to feel light-headed from inhaling paint fumes for too long. But Deeba had loved eating; she took great pleasure in preparing food and sharing it. It felt like those early dinner parties were from another lifetime, or perhaps someone else's life. When they'd first gotten together, Trina had to be trained to fit into

Deeba's health-conscious, food-oriented lifestyle, to be housebroken like a puppy. In the beginning, Deeba would send her a text that read, PLEASE GET UNSWEETENED ORGANIC NON-GMO ALMOND MILK, ORIGINAL FLAVOR. After a few weeks together, Deeba simply wrote, GET MILK.

Trina took two bites of the rapidly cooling oatmeal. She looked toward the sink full of soapy dishes, then to the algae-covered water feature, back to the countertop speckled with dried food and spilled tea and goddess knew what else. She'd clean up tomorrow. She was too tired right now. She would go back to bed, maybe turn on an old movie just to hear people talk and allow the familiar sounds to soothe her to sleep. Then, in the morning, she'd get up and really make a dent in all this mess.

She closed her eyes. Certainly there were messages from the hospital on the Electric Spirit. Who even knew if she had a job anymore. She thought about her unlimited credit stick, about how all of her needs and wants were provided for by The Seep. It wasn't like she needed a job, anyway. When Deeba first passed over, Trina had thrown herself into her work. But every healing assisted by The Seep reminded her of Deeba, how she'd chosen to leave Trina and their perfectly lovely life. She couldn't bear the platitudes of the people at the hospital—time is the only healer, it gets better, blah blah blah. Time did *not* make it better. Time made it worse, just like it made everything worse. Most horrifically of all, people expected her to be over it by now, as if her grief had a neat expiration date like the carton of milk she had left on the counter a week ago. Trina glanced into the carton, holding her nose. The milk was yellowed, congealing into little chunks. It stared at her, daring her to act. Later. She'd take care of all of it later. Tomorrow, certainly. She yawned. She needed to go back to sleep.

The bell at the front of the house rang. Trina stiffened. She wanted to hide, to lie down on her own floor amidst the empty cans and piles of books and jumbles of shoes, just so no one on the outside could glimpse her in her miserable state. Then she saw the unmistakable flash of blue outside her front window. Anger flared up, smothering her embarrassment. Trina ripped off her pajamas and pulled on jeans and a sweatshirt from a clothing pile in the living room. She opened the door.

"What the hell is this?" she said to the sweaty-looking white person shuffling on her step. He was holding a folder of blue notices in one hand and the handle of a red wagon in the other. He dropped the wagon handle and made the sign for masculine pronouns overhead. His animal familiar, a small river otter, snoozed in a shallow pool inside the wagon. "What do you think you're doing with that?" Trina asked, pointing at the blue notice. "That's not for me, is it?"

"Ms. Trina FastHorse Goldberg-Oneka?"

"Who wants to know?"

"I'm Blane. Your community seeks to address the harm you're doing. This is our third attempt at communication—"

"The harm that I'm doing? But I haven't done anything!" She barely left the house at all these days, other than to go drinking at YD's bar.

"That's exactly right. It's about what you're *not* doing. Negligence harms the community, too." He pointed to her front yard. "This was once a garden. It contributed food to the community. Now it's overgrown and gone to seed." He pressed his face against her window. "Your home itself is in desperate need of repair and cleaning."

"What warnings did I get? This is the first!"

He pointed to the massive pile of mail on the floor of Trina's hallway. "Our first communication to you about this issue was delivered via Electric Spirit. The second was handed to you by your mail volunteer." He gestured toward the blue notice in his hand. "Here is a list of all of the harmful actions you have taken, as compiled by your neighbors." His eyes were small and kind.

Trina crossed her arms and resisted the urge to slam the door in his face.

"These same neighbors," he said gently, "have offered to come help you care for your home and land, again and again." He pointed to the blue paper again. "But it's not too late! Here are some steps you could take to prove your intentions to become a caretaker."

"I've lived in this house for years," she said, closing her eyes. "I just need a little more time."

He nodded excitedly. "Yes! And you can show your intent to stay here and take care of this beautiful land by, well, taking care of it. By picking up the debris in the front yard, doing a bit of pruning—or, at the very least, by letting someone help you while you get back on your feet." The otter purred in her sleep. He bent down to scratch her behind the ear. "I've spoken with your neighbors. They've told me you're grieving." He gave her a pamphlet entitled SO, YOUR TRUE LOVE HAS BECOME A BABY . . .

Stupid fucking Seep literature, as subtle as a ton of bricks. She shoved it into her pocket.

"That's some information about grief processing and soulwork that is available to you at this time, courtesy of The Seep." He looked into her eyes. "I'd like you to know that you are not alone."

"Don't you dare tell me what I am—"

"Blane." He smiled enthusiastically, showing small, even teeth.

"All right, Blane. You know nothing about me, okay? Or what I'm going through."

He huffed in frustration, which pleased her. She wanted to crack his benevolent exterior. Why was her life his business, anyway?

"Look. You're still clearly very connected to systems

of the past." He gestured to her hoodie and jeans as if they were a political statement. Trina snorted. "But you have to get this into your head—there is no such thing as property anymore. This place isn't yours to let rot. It's an asset for the community. It was built by the energies of many different life-forms, including the trees that gave their lives for its construction, the animals that gave up their homes so yours could be built here. So if you can't take care of it, your intent to stay will lessen and dissolve."

"And then what?" Trina challenged.

He looked as if he didn't want to say the words, but he pushed on. "Then, after many more fine people like me visit you and try to get you to change your ways, a community forum will be called. And the community will decide if you are allowed to stay in this house or not. And if they decide you cannot respect this house, which they probably will, it will be given to someone else."

"Someone like you, I suppose." She looked at him sharply.

He met her gaze. "Sure. Or someone like you, Trina, before your wife changed forms. Of course, my lady and I would love a place like this. This garden must have been spectacular! Not to mention, it's meant for two people, maybe even three. Look, nothing is static. Someone lived in this place before you, and someone will live in it after you. So unpack that capitalist mind-set."

Trina felt tears pricking her eyes. "Don't fucking call me a capitalist," she said, keeping her tone flat. "And get off my porch."

"It's not *your* porch, Trina. And that's my point."

Trina fumed, her fists clenching and opening, clenching and opening. Blane held up his hands in surrender. "I'll leave. For now." He pressed a palm to the blue paper, affixing it to her door. Now everyone in the neighborhood would know her shame, know just how bad things had become.

"I hope you work things out for you, I really do." Blane picked up the handle of his little red wagon. The otter was awake now, and cleaning her paws. Blane's eyes were still warm. He paused, then said, "If you'd like, I'd be happy to stay for a little and help get you started on some of the bigger jobs—"

Trina couldn't bear a single further remark, especially one made in kindness. She slammed the door in his face.

6.

Trina stood with her back against her front door and trembled. The volunteers would be coming in droves now, a relentless stream of whole-grain casseroles, tea, and sympathy. On Saturdays, entire families might show up to help, parents and children in their little work clothes, happy and cheerful and together and not broken. Trina peered out her window. Already, there was a woman out walking with a dog (off leash, of course, because everyone knew that animals were not pets but willing companions). She saw the woman squint at the flashing blue paper, then take a few steps closer. The woman picked up a large branch that had fallen from a tree in her yard and hauled it to the side. *Oh, no she didn't*, thought Trina. *Don't you* dare! She wanted to scream at the woman, but couldn't reconcile the idea of herself literally yelling *Get off my lawn!* at a helpful stranger. Had she really become this curmudgeonly stereotype?

Trina threw on her leather jacket and boots. She grabbed the medicine bag she kept by the front door and felt her pockets for that last package of gum. Then she leaned against the wall and groaned. She used to be cool! Hip and sexy, maybe even a little bit dangerous, back when she and Horizon had toured the country, breaking hearts and getting into trouble. She looked at Deeba's old gardening shirt lying in a heap on the floor, surrounded by the detritus of their life together. She remembered Deeba in that shirt, dusty with potting soil, bringing Trina a cherry tomato warmed by the sun. Long evenings together on the back porch, watching the light change. The dinner parties they threw for friends, back before everything seemed to irritate her. Had Trina driven Deeba away? If she had been better, kinder, softer, perhaps Deeba would have stayed, and they would have been happy. Her eyes glazed over, hot with tears. She needed to cry but she couldn't, wouldn't. She couldn't stay here anymore. This place was not her home. She was drowning in filth and memories. Trina ran to the back of the house and located the never-fired gun. It had been living in the top drawer of a forgotten cabinet along with ticket stubs, rubber bands, broken vibrators, and other things Trina didn't know how to throw away. She put the gun in her bag, then ran out the front door; away from the blue sign, away from the woman and her dog, away from her messy yard, away from her problems, for they might swallow her whole if she stayed even a minute longer.

TRINA HAD JUST edged around the corner of the park where the excellent Philz Coffee still stood, proud and extraterrestrial-free, when some kid called out to her.

"Hey," the kid said. He was a pretty boy, young looking with dark brown skin and curious eyes.

"Hey yourself," said Trina, firming up her gender identity through gesture.

The boy stared down at a booklet, some kind of Seep tech that claimed to hold all the answers. These things never did, not about anything that was actually important. The Seep had the nuance of a golden retriever. All the kid seemed to want to know was a good place to stay tonight that didn't run on credit. The Seep loved giving you everything you wanted, in exchange for information about being human. The green flash of a credit stick, at a coffee shop or a bookstore or any number of places, was a marker of where you were and what you wanted, a little dot in a vast, ever-evolving data set. Trina had resigned herself to using credit years ago, to being a little dot in the aliens' matrix, but she respected the kid's wariness.

"Well, you could sleep in the park," she suggested. "But it's going to get chilly, and the grass does get dewy. There are quite a few communes who'd take you in for a night or more."

His eyes lit up. "Which commune has the most undesirable, unsavory characters?"

Trina tried not to laugh. "House of Maybe gets pretty unsavory, or at least, they used to on a Friday night. That's in Venice." Her long hand, dense with chunky silver rings, pressed into the side of a building and a blue screen appeared as if from nowhere. The boy gasped like he had never seen an Electric Spirit console before. She quickly pulled up a map and showed him which public transit lines to take to get there. "You might need a password or something—they're pretty showy—but if you bang hard enough, they'll let you in. You can say Trina Oneka sent you, but I'm not sure if my name will carry weight there anymore."

He wrote the directions down in a little notebook, real paper and all.

Trina raised her eyebrows. "You're really not from here, are you?"

He shook his head.

"If you ever have a question, just ask the pamphlet out loud. It will tell you whatever you want to know."

"What do you mean?"

"Look, I have one, too." She took out the pamphlet that busybody Blane had given her. Its title had now become SO, YOU'VE DECIDED TO RUN AWAY FROM ALL OF YOUR PROBLEMS . . . Ha, very funny. It must have overheard her conversation with Blane. "It's Seep tech. It creates a link with you, so whatever you need to know, you can find right away. It responds to verbal commands. But be wary of what you say around it—it can't always tell the difference between a question and a private conversation."

The boy stared at his pamphlet. Trina glanced at the cover. His read SO, YOU'VE BEEN EJECTED FROM THE COMPOUND . . .

Wow, thought Trina. *And I thought I had problems.* She softened her tone.

"Hey, I'm going to a diner to get some real grub. It's called The Shtetl. It doesn't use credit, either. Do you want to come?"

"No, thank you." He smiled at her, revealing shiny, straight teeth. "You see, I'm looking for something other than kindness."

"Ah," she said. "Well, maybe try Instructions? That's a commune over on Fifth." She gestured to the

map. "You could walk. They're not interested in kindness, either."

"Oh, thanks a lot!" he said brightly. Then he paused.
"Sorry. And what do I do with this?" He held out his
coffee cup. "I can't find any trash receptacles."

Trina wrinkled her brow. For someone who wasn't
interested in kindness, he sure was polite. For the
past twenty-five years, every temporary container had
been made both edible and compostable; you either
ate it or buried it in your garden. Even toddlers knew
that. Trina thought for a moment of Deeba being
raised in this new paradigm. She wouldn't remember
another way of living. Trina had to save her empty
packets of gum in a mason jar to have them processed
once a year on Old Objects New Objectives Transmutation Day. (In her former life, she might have
used the plastic packaging in an art installation about
the permanence of impermanence, but now that kind
of thing made her want to punch a wall.)

Trina made a big gesture of eating the cup, hoping
to get a smile out of him, but he only looked more
confused. Oh, well. She told him to consult the
pamphlet for little questions like that. Her gum was

starting to taste like old glue. She needed a coffee. A drink. To go to sleep and never wake up again in a world without her old lady.

The boy gave his thanks and wandered off in search of Fifth Street.

AS SOON AS he left, Trina regretted sending the kid to Instructions, a truly torturous commune that attracted the most vigilant, inflexible types looking to drop in and zone out. She wandered around the park for a while longer, frowning at the perfectly clear sky and drinking a beer in a brown paper bag. On a great open lawn, there were several yellow-meeks standing in their filthy version of prayer. Their hair was matted in clumps, faces streaked with lines of grit, necks circled in grime as they sweat and urinated on themselves in the hot overhead sun. Trina hung out with them while she finished her beer. Man, they stank! Of course, they paid her no mind, nor did they interact with each other or anyone else in the park. Over on the next field of grass, parents played with children, a teenager strummed a guitar, a middle-aged woman sunbathed in the nude. If you ignored the yellow-meeks, it was paradise. But The Seep taught us that true paradise included all of us—no matter what, no matter what, no matter what. (There was a huge living mural of this exact sentiment in the Tenderloin, depicted by hundreds of flowers and vines.) All the yellow-meeks held still, almost motionless, standing and sweating and even shitting in place when they had to, like grotesque half-alive statues. Outrageously, Trina felt sad that there were no more drunks in the park, no more homeless people except for those who had renounced housing by choice, like the yellow-meeks, who had renounced everything, even their names.

Then she berated herself for thinking such a thing. The world was better now, of course. And of course she didn't want people to suffer, unless they wanted to, even as some silly path toward divinity. She was so fucking selfish. But in that moment, she would have brought back late capitalism if it meant she were married to Deeba again. *Goddamn it*, she thought, swilling her beer. She splashed a little on her jacket and wiped it off with the back of her hand. Then she smiled. *I guess there's still one drunk in the park after all. Be the change you want to see in the world.*

Then she decided to walk to Fifth Street to try to give that Compound boy some better advice. On her walk over, Trina got more and more excited about actually talking to someone from the Compound. Was life there really free from all Seep influence? What did people tell their children about the world outside? "Hey, the Compound called," she muttered to herself as she walked through the paradise city of flowers and trees and animals with ascended consciousness. "They want their kid back."

7.

Trina was about to knock, but then she noticed that the great wooden door was slightly ajar. Knocking was for squares, anyway. She pushed the door open and walked into the massive atrium of Instructions, which was like a mansion with all its walls and doors taken away. The vast room was filled with about forty or so people of all ages, races, gender expressions, doing all manner of things. There were people fucking, of course, on beds and against walls and standing in various positions, and these larger gestures caught Trina's eye first. But then she watched for the more subtle activities. There was a general kitchen area with a small table and a freestanding stove, where a thin man was stirring an enormous pot of what smelled like tomato sauce. There was a woman frowning and clacking away at a typewriter and another playing a sort of long metal flute, while another painted her toes and sipped from a short clear glass. By a grand open window sat a man smoking as another argued with him about it, and several children ran to and fro, to and fro, around and around the room, snaking through the larger bodies and their various preoccupations. Whoever was nearby would pause what they were doing, be it meditation or armpit waxing or drawing or divination with runes, to guide the children away from an open flame or a sharp corner on a table. On the floor were the outlines of doors and walls traced in light yellow paint, a reminder of what had once been separate.

Trina didn't see the boy anywhere, or anyone she knew from the old days. In her tipsy state, she felt herself growing maudlin. *Everyone moves on.* God-damn Deeba. Leaving Trina alone in this world they had decided to walk through together.

Trina spotted a thick pamphlet on a low, sunken couch. She walked over and picked it up. It was the Seep literature the boy had been using outside of Philz Coffee. She flipped through its pages. SO, WHY DID THAT STRANGE-SMELLING MAN GROWL AT ME? SO, WHY DID MY PARENTS AND ENTIRE COMMUNITY LIE TO ME ABOUT THE OUTSIDE WORLD BEING UNINHABITABLE?

Oy vey, thought Trina. This kid was having a rough time of it.

A sallow-faced red-haired woman sat on the floor, shuffling a deck of tarot cards. She gestured toward the pamphlet. "If you're looking for that boy, he left."

"Any idea of where he was headed?"

The woman turned over a tarot card. It was The Fool. "Are you thinking of going on a quest?"

"Uh, not really. I'd like to return his pamphlet, though." She flipped it over. The back cover read SOMETIMES, PEOPLE WHO LOVE US VERY MUCH SHOW IT IN COMPLICATED WAYS. FROM YOUR PARENTS' PERSPEC-TIVE, YOU WEREN'T A PRISONER, BUT THEIR BELOVED

CHILD FOR WHOM THEY WANTED TO PROVIDE THE
SAFEST LIFE POSSIBLE, IN THE BEST WAY THEY UNDER-
STOOD HOW . . .

A sharp voice rose up from the back of the large
room. "If he left it here, why would you think he
wants you to bring it to him?"

Trina turned toward the voice. She was happy to
recognize Lydia, sitting alone at a far desk, as beautiful and as mean as ever. Not everything changed!

"Lydia!" she cried. "Why, you're as beautiful as
ever." She left out the mean part.

Lydia sat composing her unplayable music, dark
fingers moving swiftly across thick sheets of white
paper. Her newest symphony was called *Tree Mur-
derer (I Am Murdering Trees)*. Word on the street
was that everyone hated it, which seemed to be the
point.

"We may have seen your friend," said Lydia, eyes
flashing. "But we don't have to tell you anything, do
we?" She smiled, revealing teeth that narrowed into
sharp little points.

Trina felt oddly moved by Lydia's whole deal—
her rudeness, her general fuck-you to this cheery,

wearying world. "Lydia," she said. "I love you. Should we get married?"

Lydia snorted. "Nice try. I'm not about to let you oppress me with your systems of heteronormativity, stud." She slashed a long, dark line through the paper, bisecting the carefully notated music. "This piece is ruined!" Then she tossed her thick braids. "Now it's perfect."

"Ooh, I've missed you!" Trina laughed. "Please never change."

Lydia gazed at Trina with flinty, unblinking eyes. "That's a very cruel thing to ask of anyone."

Trina felt exposed suddenly, as if she were naked in the middle of Instructions (which wouldn't have been a problem: a few people were. Trina noticed a man sitting on the toilet and another woman in the giant bathtub, scrubbing her back with a long wooden brush).

Lydia looked at her, her eyes steady. "And I won't be your rebound, Trina." Her voice was almost gentle. "Get thee to a therapist, babe."

"Damn, Lydia," said the redhead. "Even for you, that's cold." She turned over another tarot card, and then another. It was the Nine of Cups, followed by the Queen of Cups reversed. "Go check your favorite bar. You'll find him there." She looked up at Trina with watery pale eyes. "And interrogate the depth of your sadness or you'll drown."

Trina left Instructions without another word to anyone. *I don't need a therapist*, she thought. *I need a goddamn drink.*

She squeezed both pamphlets in her pocket. She liked holding them together. She would find this boy. This lost boy who was in terrible need, in terrible pain. They had so much in common, he and she. The boy from the bubble and the woman who refused to move on. He had been betrayed by the people who claimed to love him, and so had she. She thought back to the tarot card of The Fool. She smiled. Nothing wrong with being a little foolish. It kept you young.

ON A BENCH outside The Shtetl, a young woman of Japanese descent sat holding a bucket of tiny fish. She took one in her hand, placed the whole wriggling fish into her mouth, and started to chew. Then she started crying, sobbing, as if her beloved had died. She kept crying and eating, eating and crying over the tiny fish one by one. Trina felt moved by the depth of her sadness, which seemed to mirror her own. She sat down next to the woman on the bench.

"Hey," said Trina.

The woman kept on eating and crying. "Hello," she said, still actively sobbing. "How are you today?"

"I'm okay," Trina said. "How are you?"

"I'm very, very sad," the woman said while chewing and swallowing, chewing and swallowing.

"Oh?" Trina turned toward her. She felt her own sadness pile up in her throat, squeezing her like a tight collar, then more like a noose. "Would you like to talk about it?"

"Sure," she said, wiping her nose. "I'm just so sad about the death of all these fishes." She took another murderous bite. "They just don't stand a chance."

Trina shuddered and stood up. Behind her, the woman sobbed louder and louder.

8.

Trina walked inside the nondescript off-white building just as it was starting to rain. The sign read:

YOUR HOMELAND DOESN'T EXIST
ANYMORE!
SO GET OVER IT, BABE

in cheery pink bubble letters. Inside, the small

restaurant was dim. There was a long wooden bar with stools, and tables and dark booths hugging the corners. An ancient-looking woman stood behind the bar, wiping down glasses. Good old YD. Trina sighed. Some things really never did change. Her hair was still cropped in a tight buzz cut, and she wore her white cotton T-shirt and one long, dangling earring like a uniform. The restaurant was pretty empty of patrons, just a couple cooing over a bassinet with an orange kitten swaddled in baby blankets inside it. Trina didn't see the boy anywhere.

"*Nu?*" asked YD, gesturing at her with a dishrag. "You don't call, you don't write. I didn't know what happened to you!"

"Hey, momma," said Trina, leaning over to kiss her old wrinkled cheek. "I fell into a black hole for a few days. Took me a little while to climb out."

YD's lips puckered into a frown. Trina squeezed her hand. It hadn't occurred to her that YD would worry. "I'm sorry. I'll do better next time."

"Okay, okay." YD nodded. "What can I get you, *mameleh?*"

"The daily special, please, and thank you." She

smiled at YD sweetly. "And the best cocktail in the world?"

"*Mameleh*, is that a good idea?"

"YD, I'm fine! I just feel like having a cocktail, okay?"

"Okay, okay." She looked into Trina's eyes. "You had us all a little worried, Trinelah. My mind went to all the bad places."

Trina laughed. "YD, your mind always goes to the worst possible scenario, no matter what I do."

YD smiled. "I'm part of a long, grand tradition of worriers."

"You could have reached out to me, you know."

YD waved her hand overhead. "You know I don't like to bother you. You're busy!" She began fixing the drink. "With the hospital. You're a very important lady!"

Trina smiled. YD was feeling guilty. She could get two, maybe even three drinks out of her tonight without too much hassle. For a society built around "live and let live," everyone sure liked getting into Trina's business. No one needed to know she hadn't been to work in months. Anyway, she had more important things to do. Someone needed her help. She had to find that kid from the Compound.

YD DIDN'T GIVE her too hard of a time, but Pina the bear wasn't impressed. She trundled out from the kitchen on her hind legs, holding the daily special carefully. She was generally a pretty grumpy bear, and she had been in an especially bad mood since the summer. Pina gave Trina one long look, her paws gripping the plate like big leather gloves. "You smell like poison," Pina grunted before dropping YD's delicious *kasha varnishkes* down with a bang. It was a miracle she hadn't broken all of YD's dishes.

Trina took a big sip off the top of her Old-Fashioned. It ran down her gullet in a bright line. YD certainly knew how to make a cocktail. "I love you, YD!" She took another little slurp. "I love you so much," she whispered to her drink.

Pina came over with a tall glass of water. "Here. You drunk already."

"Don't oppress me with your old-fashioned moralizing, man," said Trina.

Pina frowned at her. "Stop using words to confuse me." She lumbered back to the kitchen. "And I'm not a man!"

"Well, neither am I." Bears were so literal. Trina sucked at her drink. The edges of the world were already starting to blur nicely. "You smell like a wet dog, ever think of that?" she muttered softly. One had to be careful. Pina's depth perception wasn't great, but her hearing was top-notch.

Trina got up to pay her water bill. What a stupid way of saying she had to pee. If she said that to one of those Seep kids, they'd probably ask her if she was talking about the old days of scarcity mentality. Before the arrival of The Seep, she and Deeba would earnestly talk about the heady ideal of a world without money. Trina hadn't known what kind of revolution she wanted; she had trouble deciding what to eat for breakfast. Deeba had always been more militant and exacting in her demands of the world. How she had loved Deeba's fierce certainty. *Goddamn Deeba*, thought Trina. *Leaving me here by myself in this* fakakta *future!* Trina splashed her face with cold water. She was starting to sound like YD.

Trina heard a rustling from outside the restaurant, like something rooting around in the trash. She looked out of the little bathroom window onto the back alley. It was the kid from the Compound! Bless that creepy redhead and her silly tarot cards. Magic was real, Blessed Be! The boy was just wandering around the alley, looking lost. Trina watched as he took a few steps, then stopped and walked back, as if unsure of what direction to go in or whether he wanted to reach his destination at all.

Another figure approached from the main street, cutting through the alley toward the boulevard. It was Horizon Line, that cheap hack of a performance artist! She hadn't seen him in years, not since that silly dinner party. Trina watched as Horizon approached the boy. A coil of rage unspooled in her belly. Trina wanted to punch the wall. Her fists clenched in anticipation of doing so, but then she thought about how sad YD would be if she actually hurt The Shtetl. It was so annoying to know that even buildings could feel pain. Of course, The Shtetl didn't deserve any of her ire. She relaxed her hands. But goddamn it, Horizon was still wearing that dead man's face! From the looks of him, he had gotten a few other Seep mods in the past few years—some silly deer ears, hair extensions. He and the boy talked for a few moments before Horizon took the boy's hand and led him to the boulevard. Perhaps the boy had found what he was looking for after all. Horizon Line was certainly not kind.

Still, Trina didn't like the idea of him with the kid. She and the boy from the Compound had both lost people they loved, both been betrayed by the whole damn world. *She* should be the one taking him by the hand, not Horizon Line. He needed someone older and wiser who could help him find his footing in this strange new place.

Trina surged toward the door, then stumbled, banging her knee into a wall. *Oh, shit.* She was pretty drunk. No matter. She ran out the back door and into the alley. She could see Horizon Line's dark antlered head moving down the wide lush street alongside the boy's. She raised her hand and started to call out to stop them. But just then, a herd of deer clipped down the street, followed by a topless unicycle collective. Trina stood on her tiptoes, trying to get a glimpse of which direction Horizon and the boy had gone, but they were lost behind the crowd. The dust settled. She saw the dense plant life on the street repairing itself from the deer hooves and unicycle treads. Trina grimaced and rubbed her knee, then looked at her hand and realized it was lightly smeared with blood. She hobbled back toward The Shtetl. Okay, there was more than one way to pet a cat. So medical attention first, then she'd go find the boy. And give Horizon Line a piece of her mind, too. She had intended to tell everyone about what he had done to that poor young man, stealing his face after his death. Why hadn't she gone through with it?

Then the order of events came rushing toward her like an oncoming train. Because she had been too distracted by Deeba wanting to become a child again, by the love of her life leaving her alone in this miserable paradise.

She fingered the gum packet. Only ten pieces left.

But then Trina smiled, even though her knee hurt like hell. Because suddenly, she didn't feel like hiding at The Shtetl forever or throwing herself into the sea.

"Barkeep!" Trina called as she walked back inside. "I need one more drink while I formulate my secret plan." All she had so far was (1) Find the boy, and (2) Punch Horizon Line's pretty stolen face instead of a wall. The rest of the details she would work out later. Right now, Trina needed another cocktail, and maybe to rest her eyes for a bit.

9.

Trina blinked her eyes open, her head slumped in her arms on top of the bar. Her drink was half-full and warm in front of her. She drank it gratefully. Trina took out the pamphlet she had gotten from Blane. Its title had changed again. Now it read:

SO, YOU'RE THINKING OF GOING ON A

VENGEFUL QUEST . . .

Trina snorted. "Oh my," she said. "Well, aren't you clever." She flipped open the booklet. It seemed thicker than before. She patted her pockets for the second pamphlet, the one she had to return to the boy. It wasn't in any of them. Had she dropped it?

SO, YOU'RE THINKING OF GOING ON A VENGEFUL QUEST! WE APPLAUD YOUR PASSION AND YOUR CONVICTION, AND WE RECOGNIZE THAT YOU HAVE A LOT TO BE HURT AND ANGRY ABOUT. YOU HAVE EVERY RIGHT TO FEEL ALL KINDS OF EMOTIONS! WHAT AN AMAZING PART OF BEING A HUMAN BEING.

Trina snorted. "Gee, thanks."

BUT CONSIDER YOUR END GOAL HERE. HURTING SOMEONE WHO'S HURT YOU WILL ONLY CREATE MORE HURT. HOW CAN WE HELP YOU FEEL BETTER IN A MORE PRODUCTIVE FASHION?

Trina gritted her teeth. "You have the emotional intelligence of a motivational poster," she said.

THAT HURTS OUR FEELINGS!

"You don't have feelings," said Trina.

The pamphlet's words melted together into a big frowny face. Trina shoved it into her jacket pocket.

TRINA SAT AT the bar stool with her medicine bag in her lap. Deeba used to call it her "Mary Poppins bag," as it always seemed to contain whatever they needed.

The bag wasn't all that magical. True, there was a bit of Seep tech sewn into its design, so Trina's hand quickly grabbed whatever it was looking for, and no matter how many objects she accumulated, it remained light and portable. But along with actual medical supplies, Trina had carried things for her wife, like packets of nuts for when Deeba felt peckish or little gloves for her often cold hands, so to her wife it *had* seemed like a magic bag.

These objects were useless now. Trina wasn't about to eat any five-year-old cashews or wrestle her big hands into fuzzy little gloves, but she couldn't bear to throw them away, to see them get sucked back into the ground, bound to endlessly cycle through other uses in unknown places. Trina reached into the medicine bag past the trinkets from her previous life, past the small jars of salves and creams, past packets of biodegradable gloves, bandages and rubbing alcohol, to feel the cold, hard gun at the very bottom. The bag did not offer the gun up to her, as it did with the other objects it held. But the gun felt good, and the searching for it felt good, too. She was going on a goddamn quest! She hadn't been on a quest in ages. It was a good thing she was wearing boots.

A feeling bloomed inside of Trina's chest. She wasn't just going to stick it to Horizon Line, that no-good Seep artist. She was going to save that poor Compound kid. He was so lost, so clueless. He needed her and he didn't even know it. Sometimes, you have to show people that they need help before it's too late. YD came back in, holding a toe in a little glass jar.

Trina cleared her throat. "YD, are you decomposing again?"

"Not as bad as all that." YD batted her eyes innocently. "I just need my toe reattached."

Trina sat YD down and started massaging her swollen ankles. "You have to let me do a bigger healing job on you, old girl."

"Sure, sure, one of these days." YD's tone was light. "*Mamelah*, I was strolling through the Mission today and I thought I might stop by for a cup of tea . . ."

"You were checking up on me?" Trina groaned.

"You hadn't been around for a while! I thought maybe something was wrong. And then I saw the blue sign." YD hissed as Trina reattached the toe. "Ooh, that stings!" She flexed her newly attached toes and smiled. "Thanks, friend."

Trina rubbed the resinous tip of her Seep wand into the broken flesh of her own knee. Already her cells were knitting back together, just like how the plant life had repaired itself on the road after that herd of deer and unicycles. *The Seep wants nothing more than to kiss our boo-boos away,* Trina thought derisively. She could feel the lightest sensation of its alien presence in her bloodstream. She really should stop drinking so much. She knew she was destroying her liver, not to mention wreaking havoc on her circulatory system. And her sleep cycle was so out of whack, she never felt fully rested . . .

Then she scowled and clutched her drink defiantly. Who was to say what was best for anyone else? She swallowed hard. The warm cocktail now tasted like poison, but she'd push through. She'd done it before, and she'd do it again. Trina drank more, and this time she was able to find a little bit of pleasure in that old familiar place. Deeba had hated the rare occasions when Trina overindulged in liquor. She'd be so shocked to see her now. Trina took yet another sip. This gave her a new kind of pleasure, a sense of power. She was becoming a different person, unrecognizable as the one Deeba had left behind. *Serves her right.*

YD sighed. She took Trina's face in her wrinkled hands. "I love you, kiddo. It breaks my heart to see you languishing like this. What can I do? Tell me."

Pina came up behind them and made her friendliest growl.

YD put her arms around them both. "That's right. Pina, too! How can we help?"

Trina shrugged. The world was starting to get blurry again. Stupid Deeba. Leaving her to become an alcoholic. It was *her* fault, really. Trina couldn't be blamed for it. "You can make me another drink."

Pina sucked in through her long teeth. "We love you, and you spit on our love."

Trina put a hand on Pina's and YD's shoulders. "Geez, okay. Listen, YD, can I stay here tonight? Then I'm going to go away, for maybe a day or two, maybe a little longer. There's something I have to do. But when I come back, I'll deal with my shit. I promise. I just need to do this one thing. Then everything will be better, trust me." Trina smiled. She almost believed it herself.

"And what's this mysterious task, dare I ask?"

Trina wrinkled her nose. "I'd prefer that you didn't."

YD waved her hand in the air. "Fine, fine. Stay here tonight, of course you can stay. Bunk with me, though. Pina howls in her sleep."

Trina closed her eyes and saw the flash of blue on her front door. It would feel so good to get away from it all. "And may I please have a little drink? A baby one?"

Pina growled a decidedly unfriendly growl.

YD groaned, but Trina could tell she had already given in. "You *meshugana* girl, I can't say no to you." Pina whined at YD, but she ignored it. She shuffled back behind the bar and took out a bottle of bourbon from a high shelf. She muddled cherries and oranges in the bottom of a rocks glass for an Old-Fashioned. The instant Trina saw YD put her hands on the bottle, she felt safe.

10.

Happily buzzed and pleasantly warm, Trina fiddled with her Electric Spirit console until she found Horizon's channel. There were dozens of videos: clips of performances, little interviews. She tapped on the one with the highest number of views. It was titled "A Treatise on the Transmutation of Objects, or Welcome to Possibility!"

Horizon, gorgeous and severe in a gossamer sheath

of black and gray, looked directly at the camera. "Hi, beautiful people," he said. "Today is November second, 2037, on the Earth plane in this linear construct we call time." He ran a hand through his hair and it shimmered, catching the light like silk. Pina grunted and shifted behind Trina, negotiating her bulk closer so she could see the screen, too.

"This video is coming to you from The Kitchen, a performance space very near and dear to my heart, in what was once called Tucson." He took a sip from a glass of fizzy water and cleared his throat. "The main message I have for you today is that we don't yet know what to call ourselves, as both human beings and as symbionts of The Seep. Seamlessly and elegantly, we've adjusted to this new way of living, and we should celebrate ourselves and The Seep for the ease of that merger. As you all know, The Seep has improved our lives in myriad ways—personal and public, political and private. I could name a dozen different ways this happened just off the top of my head, and I'm sure you could, too. Feel free to mention the ways The Seep has affected your life in the chat below." He smiled at the camera, revealing long front teeth. It was disarming; a pretty vampire. "So! No one is denying the effects of The Seep in furthering human consciousness, health, and freedom. But I *do* wonder if we've become lazy in our own use of The Seep." He stared deeply into the camera, eyes wet and sincere. "Think back to your first Seep experience. So profound, so meaningful. And now we're surrounded by our alien friends day in, day out. They make us healthier, our streets more beautiful, our plants more bountiful. We know that The Seep wants nothing but to make us happy, and in return, to experience the pleasures of embodied form, the delightful relief of linear time. I'm not questioning the intentions of The Seep like some of the folks you'll find here, broadcasting their conspiracy theories on the Electric Spirit. But again, I *do* think we've become too complacent in our interactions with it. The Seep continues to give us what it thinks we want: health, abundance, community, freedom. But! Let us not be yoked to the desires of our predecessors. Theirs was a world of scarcity, artificial competition, and fear. Our future-present is exceedingly lush, but we must not let this bounty distract us from aiming even higher. Remember, only a few dozen years ago, the idea of life without death was laughable, more at home in comic books than scientific journals. I assert that we have just begun to discover the potential collaborations between human and Seep forms. A world of unknown possibilities is waiting for us. But enough talk," he said. "Let me show you what I mean."

Horizon took out an old-fashioned-looking gold pocket watch and set it down in the center of a long table. Then he took out his Seep wand and coated his hands thickly with its resinous tip. Trina wanted to know how Horizon Line had gotten his grubby hands on a medical-grade Seep wand more suited to surgery than performance art. His hands glowed blue in the camera light. Horizon closed his eyes and concentrated, mouthing a stream of words under his breath. He picked up the gold watch with both hands and held it still, as if trapping a tiny animal. His words turned into a high whistle, an ethereal sound like someone playing the saw. Horizon rubbed his hands together, squeezing the gold watch between his glowing palms. The whistling turned into a resonant hum. He pressed and squeezed the watch, turning the mass in his hands. A thick gray feather flared up from between his clasped palms. He kept on humming and rotating his closed hands. Then they began to vibrate, his arms to shake and shiver. A current, like an electric shock, ran through his whole body, but he kept his hands tight around the form. A squawk sounded out. Horizon Line looked straight at the camera and opened his hands.

It was a small golden bird, flitting to and fro. The camera followed its erratic, disoriented flight. The bird didn't seem too happy about being born, but who didn't cry on their way into the world? The gold bird settled on a high shelf, and the camera panned in close on its black blinking eye. Then its head turned sharply to reveal a round metal gear embedded into one side of its round head. The magical mechanical bird squawked once more before the camera returned to Horizon's flushed face. "I'm Horizon Line," he said. "Performer, thinker, Seep Alchemist. I have turned gold into life." He wiped his brow. "As human beings, we still have no concept of what we really are. This world is so much more than you could ever imagine. Therefore, I ask you— what will you make today?" He smiled wide into the camera. "If you liked this video, please hit 'Subscribe' on the Electric Spirit so you can follow my future adventures in transformation. Bye for now." He blew a kiss, and the screen went black.

"HE GIVES ME the willies," said Pina slowly. "Am I saying that right? He makes my skin feel creepy-crawly. I don't like it."

"Me too, Pina, my dear," said Trina. "Me too."

Pina frowned. "I'm not a deer, I'm a bear." Then she smiled, a horrifying display of glistening teeth. "I made a joke. Get it?"

11.

Trina discovered Horizon would be playing the next night at The Go-Go, one of Trina's favorite venues from the old days. She registered for the 11 A.M. high-speed bullet train to Detroit. Eventually, Pina put away her mop with a bang and growled at Trina to call it a night. Last call had been hours ago, and YD was probably long asleep.

TRINA LIGHTLY KNOCKED on YD's bedroom door and crawled in next to her. It felt nice to lie next to a smelly, snoring body. She wasn't worried about finding Horizon and the boy. It was easy enough to find someone. But that didn't mean you could get them to do what you wanted or even understand what you were trying to say. Talking was easy. Communication was hard. She thought back to the gun, her destroyer of worlds. Maybe the time for talking was over. If she shot Horizon Line, he wouldn't really be dead. No one ever died, she now knew, they just became something else. Still. That was the logic of a sociopath. If she shot Horizon Line, the person she'd really be killing was herself, her old self. She'd no longer be Trina, the person who would never fire a gun at someone. She thought again about how Deeba wouldn't recognize her now, unkempt and rugged, leather jacket smelling of old beer. If she killed Horizon Line, she'd be killing Deeba's wife. Was that an act she was ready to commit?

Next to her, YD shifted and yawned. "All that drinking is ruining your sleep," she said pleasantly.

"I know, momma." Trina could hear the revelers

leaving the club down the street, ready to stumble to their beds. "YD," she said quietly. "When are you going to die?"

YD reached under the sheet and found Trina's hand. She gave it a squeeze. "Not anytime soon, *shayna punim.*"

"Living on and on while everyone you love changes . . . Doesn't that make you sad?"

YD scoffed. "You people, you think happiness is the only important thing about being alive. I'm serious when I say I'm not interested in happiness. This old body hurts. That's as worthy an experience as any."

Sounds of laughter came up from the street, mixed with off-tune singing of something like "L'Internationale."

"I am interested in death, though. I think it's going to be a grand adventure. I hope I get to stay dead, at least for a little while, before I become something else. I've heard there's a whitish period, and then everything turns red, and then you sink into lovely blackness." She laughed and flicked Trina's leg. "Now go to sleep."

Trina was still thinking about death's colors when sleep welled up and pulled her under.

THAT NIGHT, TRINA dreamt that her father was telling a long, confusing joke. She had missed the setup, which didn't help, but the joke kept expanding every minute until it contained dozens of characters and scenarios. She reached out to put her hand on his shoulder, to say hey, enough is enough. But as she touched him, Trina realized he was a sack containing other people. He leaned in toward her, opening his mouth wide. His throat was a black hole. He wasn't her father at all, just someone wearing his skin. She tried to get away, but her feet were stuck in place. The black hole of his gaping mouth filled her vision until it was all she could see, like an expanse of unending horizon.

12.

Trina's train was crowded with reservations. The only empty seats were in a church service. A short woman with thick black hair played the keyboard and swayed in time to the music. A tall person of ambiguous gender played the flute, tapping their foot in time.

A very short man stood in front of a low microphone and spoke softly, his whispers amplified around the train car. "There are a lot of things I still miss," he said. "I miss talking to my mom on the phone. We'd have a call every Sunday. It gave my life a special consistency. She didn't commit suicide when the aliens came; she was already in assisted living by then. But she did die in those early confusing months, when we couldn't be certain if the world was really ending." His whispers grew faster. "I think I'm a lot like you, with loved ones who decided that it was the time to depart when the world got too weird. So I think of my mother, on this Sunday, when we would have had our weekly call. And I think of my future self, when I've lived long enough to forget our Sunday ritual, and perhaps even what the word *Sunday* means. And I offer you, and myself, this prayer."

The congregation joined in, a roomful of voices mumbling together. "I am all the things I don't know. Everything is unfolding as it should, and that doesn't mean I can't be mad about it."

The short man broke out into a broad grin. "Great, everyone!" He squinted around the train car. "I see some new faces this morning. That's just wonderful. Everyone, introduce yourself to your neighbor. Shake hands, if that's a comfortable practice for you. Say something you miss about Before." The congregation broke out into little murmuring groups. Trina suddenly wished she were standing in the café car, drinking bad coffee. Anywhere but here.

An older woman reached across the aisle to shake Trina's hand. "Hi, I'm Betty," she said. "I really miss Cheetos. They were so crunchy and brightly colored, and they made my fingers glow orange. I know it's better that we don't eat highly processed foods containing a variety of chemicals and, oh God, red or yellow dye, but I really do miss them." She smiled. "And you?"

"Um, I'm Trina," she said. She tried to answer the woman's question truthfully. "I miss cheeseburgers," she said slowly. "We would get them on Saturday, after soccer practice—my brother, my father, and I. They were wrapped in paper. They tasted good when they were hot and bad when they were cold. I know it's murder to eat other animals now, but I still miss them." Trina felt her throat grow tight. Deeba had been a vegan long before the aliens came. Some people didn't need cosmic intervention to know how to be good.

Trina stood, rocking slightly from the motion of the high-speed train. "Excuse me," she said. She walked through the rest of the church service to go stand in the café car. As she walked, she overheard other people sharing memories of life Before.

"Hi Sandra," said a dark-skinned man with a smooth, shiny head. "I'm Edwin, but most people call me Eddie. Right now, I'm thinking about my family's all-day barbecues at the beach. Grandma would practically bring her whole apartment. Chairs, tents to block the sun, tables and tables of food. We'd set up in the morning and stay until well after dark. I miss the smell of sunscreen, my uncles competing over the grill, the sound of my mother's wonderful laugh . . ."

IN THE CAFÉ car, Trina scowled into her coffee. She just didn't understand the world anymore. How could you worship change and worship the past at the same time? It just didn't make any sense. She took out a little flask from her jacket and made her coffee Irish. That turned her frown upside down.

She looked at the pamphlet. "Hey, Pam," she

CHANA PORTER

murmured. "I hope you don't mind, I've decided to call you Pam. It's short for pamphlet, get it?"

Red hearts appeared, exploding over the cover. WE THINK YOUR SENSE OF HUMOR IS VERY FUN! THANK YOU FOR OUR NICKNAME!

Trina snorted. "You have a lot to learn, kiddo."

WE CERTAINLY HOPE SO! LEARNING IS OUR FAVORITE THING.

She drank more spiked coffee. "Hey, Pam. I'm having a brainstorm. I don't think I dropped that Compound kid's pamphlet. I think you ate it, or you merged into one, or whatever."

THAT'S CORRECT, TRINA. WE ARE VERY LUCKY TO HAVE CONNECTED TO TWO SUCH UNIQUE EXPERIENCES. WE ARE A TRULY UNIQUE PAMPHLET!

"That's interesting, Pam," said Trina. The rapidity of its communication with her was certainly new, as was this conversational tone. "Has this ever happened before?" The doctor in her wanted to do an experiment. Her fingers itched to take out her Seep wand and poke around, but she didn't want to get high.

OTHER SEEP LITERATURE HAS MERGED TOGETHER AFTER ITS READERS HAVE BONDED WITH THEIR

PAMPHLETS AND ONE ANOTHER—BUT THIS HAS NEVER HAPPENED UNTIL NOW WITH ONE WHO HAS BEEN RAISED IN THE COMPOUND, FREE OF ALL SEEP INFLUENCE, AND ONE WHO HAS LIVED AMONGST THE SEEP FOR AS LONG AS YOU HAVE, TRINA.

Trina raised an eyebrow. "I see. You're calling me old."

THE AGE OF YOUR FLESH-BODY IS RELEVANT IN THIS CIRCUMSTANCE, YES! BUT, ABOUT WHAT YOU WERE PONDERING AFTER THE CHURCH SERVICE—WE HAVE AN IDEA, TRINA, OF WHY HUMANS ARE OBSESSED WITH BOTH THE PAST AND FUTURE AT THE SAME TIME. MAY WE SHARE OUR THOUGHT WITH YOU?

Trina blinked. "You mean, you have a thought to share with me about the thought I was having and didn't verbalize? You can read my mind now?" She realized it had already done that once before, at The Shtetl, but she had been too shitfaced to notice. *So you're thinking of going on a vengeful quest . . .*

All this drinking really was dulling her mind. She pushed the coffee away. Then she pulled it back and took another sip.

YES, IT'S MUCH FASTER THIS WAY. HERE'S OUR IDEA,

TRINA, ABOUT WHY HUMANS ARE SO FOCUSED ON THE PAST AND THE FUTURE, ALL AT ONCE. IT'S ABOUT LEARNING! THAT'S THE GREAT GIFT OF LINEAR TIME! YOU CAN LOOK BACK ON YOUR EXPERIENCES IN THE PAST AND USE THEM TO MAKE CHOICES FOR THE FUTURE. TIME IS EMBODIED LEARNING! THAT'S WHY MEMORY EXISTS! WHY FAILURES ARE NEVER TRULY FAILURES, AND MISTAKES ARE ALWAYS GLORIOUS! NO MATTER WHAT, NO MATTER WHAT, NO MATTER WHAT, NO MATTER WHAT!

Little explosions of color danced across the paper like a tiny fireworks display.

Trina grunted. "You might have a point there." Would she have gotten together with Deeba, all those years ago, if she had known the pain it would cause her in the future? Perhaps not. But now that she'd had them, she wouldn't trade anything for those years. Maybe knowledge of the future would have changed the outcome, but who was to say?

DO YOU WANT US TO TELL YOU?

Trina felt the tears coming. Her body was betraying her yet again. But she shook them away. "No. I don't want to know." She could drown like this, gaming out possible scenarios with an all-knowing oracle that just wanted to make her happy. The Seep was like a child, growing every day, with such a limited understanding of human complexity. Trina could lose herself in its sloppy benevolence.

WHAT ARE YOU GOING TO DO WITH THAT GUN, TRINA?

"None of your goddamn business, Pam." She shoved the pamphlet into her bag.

13.

Trina got off the train and looked at the open sky. She fucking loved Detroit. The former factories in the city center were now dense centers of permaculture; massive, wild farms dotted with coffee shops, restaurants, collective housing, schools, and squats. It was Deeba who had wanted to live in the Bay Area. Maybe this whole silly quest was some kind of sign that it was time to see what else was out there. Maybe even this Detroit was too familiar. The whole world was available to Trina; she could live on a riverboat or a cave in Peru or any of a million other places. Trina pushed a piece of gum out from the packet, but instead of putting it in her mouth, she let it fall. The gum just lay there, inert and frozen on the ground. It couldn't be taken back into the earth. Some things never really went away. Maybe she was like that, too, a relic from another time, unable to exist in the framework of the new. Stubborn, useless, unwanted. She squeezed the pamphlet in her pocket. It was hot to the touch, like a child's feverous forehead.

"What the fuck?" Trina asked no one in particular. She did not like what was happening. But she took the bait and pulled out the pamphlet.

TRINA, YOU ARE SO WANTED AND LOVED RIGHT NOW, IN THIS EXACT MOMENT! BY OLD FRIENDS YOU HAVEN'T SEEN IN A LONG TIME, BY STRANGERS YOU HAVE NEVER EVEN MET! IT'S EACH OF US TOGETHER THAT MAKES OUR SUM TOTAL, OUR WHOLE. EVERYONE IS NEEDED, EXACTLY AS THEY ARE.

"Pam," groaned Trina. "What's going on here?

You're summoning me now? After reading my mind? For these little pep talks?"

The pamphlet was blank for a long while.

"Well?!"

Then, a tiny voice spoke. *"We thought,"* the voice said, *"you might prefer the change in temperature to actually being spoken to. Were we wrong?"*

Trina froze, her hands and feet gone cold.

"No, no," said the pamphlet. *"Don't be scared. There's nothing to be frightened of, Trina! We love you!"*

Trina's hands felt huge, the pamphlet light and heavy in her palm at the same time.

Text appeared on the pamphlet once more. WE ARE VERY SORRY WE SCARED YOU, TRINA! WE WON'T TALK AGAIN UNLESS YOU ASK US TO.

IN THE EARLY afternoon, Trina reached The Go-Go, a former firehouse in the middle of a well-sized farm. The main house was divided between residencies and the performance venue, but the collective expanded out over the surrounding land, with some members living in tiny houses along the perimeter. Someone was practicing drums in a yurt, while an older man hung laundry outside on a clothesline. A person of ambiguous gender sat with a young child in their arms, reading a book out loud under a tree. In her heyday, Trina had loved crashing at The Go-Go during her tours, adding her name to the meal roster in the kitchen, grateful for a bowl of lentil curry and relaxed conversation. Maybe she would crash here for a while once she found this kid. Maybe they could rest here together until she figured out her next move.

There was a dragon at the door to the performance space, one of those tough types who'd used all kinds of Seep mods to make their body fierce and frightening—scaly skin, yellow, reptilian eyes, muscles for miles, that kind of thing. Trina ignored the dragon and walked up to the ticket booth. Her dear friend from the old touring days, Bartleby, was still there in his big plastic glasses, nose deep in a book. A little balder, a little haggard now, but still the same Bartleby. Trina felt deeply comforted by the sight of him. *Some things in the world don't change.*

She leaned on the counter. "Hey, man, you gonna give your old friend a hug, or would you prefer not to?"

Bartleby put down the tattered Delany paperback and stared up at her. "Aw, FastHorse!" He shuffled out from behind the little ticket booth to give her a squeeze. The top of his head came up to her neck. She grinned, feeling suddenly more optimistic than she had all year. "Aw, geez, it's good to see you, man."

"Did I get the line right? It's been ages!"

He shook his head. "These kids today, they're goddamn illiterates. No one reads books anymore; they just merge with trees for kicks." He squeezed her again, then backed away to look at her. "Aw, Trina, you really look great. It's been years, hasn't it? Man, time flies when you're immortal. That is, when it isn't staying completely still."

"I wasn't sure I'd find you here, Bart. You're still doing the same thing?"

"What can I say? I love a routine!" He smiled. "These young folks keep me spry. And there's always someone from the old days coming through, so that's nice." He looked behind her. "Where's Deeba?" Before Trina could think of what to say, Bartleby clicked his tongue. "Oh, I see. She moved on?"

"Yeah," said Trina. "I still can't believe it. I wake up in the morning and I think she's there."

"That's harsh, man. How long were you together?"

"Twenty-five years."

"Did you have a funeral for her?"

Trina bobbed her head. She didn't tell Bartleby she hadn't attended.

"Oof, that's rough." Bartleby sighed. "Everyone is itching to become someone else. These kids today, they don't know anything about commitment. When Petra died . . . man, I thought I'd never love again. But unfortunately, life moves on. I'm still married to her memory, though. But you gotta figure out how to be in the present." He smiled at her. Petra's body had been destroyed in a rock-climbing accident. She had been too far gone to be healed by The Seep, her essence lost, tangled somewhere in the earth. No one knew what she would become, or if she would remember her past life. These kinds of sudden, violent body deaths were rare, but they did still happen. The path Deeba had chosen was very different.

"I can't talk about this with you," Trina said quietly, looking away. "At least, definitely not sober."

She found her flask in her pocket and just pressed it, finding comfort in its cool, familiar metal against her fingers.

He squinted at her. "Forgive me," he said, lightly touching the back of her hand. "I don't know what I'm talking about. What have you been doing with yourself?"

Trina assumed a cocky pose, her hand on a hip jutting out to the side. "I'm a doctor now."

"Aw, man, that's so cool." He beamed at her. "Maybe I'll do a real one-eighty someday, too, you know? Like learn to play chess or master an instrument or write the great post-American novel."

"We got plenty of time." She cleared her throat. "Listen, Bart. I heard Horizon was playing tonight. Can you find me a pass?"

Bartleby grinned and cracked his knuckles. "Of course!" He went back into his little booth and logged on to the Electric Spirit. "How many do you need?"

"It's just me."

"Let's see, let's see, reservations . . ."

His voice trailed off. Bartleby looked up past Trina to the dragon by the door, then back to the screen, scrolling vaguely. "Sorry, babe! I didn't realize we were completely at capacity tonight. But!" He banged his hand on his little table. "Tonight in the lounge, we have Hmong death ritual poetry by Shan Hou. I'm going to that myself." He glanced toward the dragon. "I don't much care for Horizon's new direction, honestly. And I don't think you will either."

Trina leaned in close. "Is that so?"

He blinked up at her. "Yeah. I find it . . . problematic."

"Well, I'm sure I'll agree with you, but I'd like to judge that for myself. Is Horizon here? I'm sure if I could speak with him, he'd put me on the list." Trina wasn't so certain. They hadn't spoken since their fight in the garden all those years ago. But he'd probably love that she was groveling to see his latest work.

His eyes brightened. "Hey, you know what? I haven't had a night off in ages. No Hmong poetry, no performance art—why don't we go get dinner? Like, just the two of us?" He blushed. "There's something I want to show you."

"I'd like that," said Trina slowly. Something about this was very wrong. She'd happily have dinner with Bart any day. They'd always gotten along swimmingly, particularly now that no one cared about books and records anymore unless they had been made by Seeped swarms of bees or whatever else the kids were into these days. But it made no sense that he wouldn't squeeze her into the show. At one of Trina's last performances at The Go-Go, the crowd had been so big that they'd just moved outside and performed in a field. There was something fishy afoot. "I'm sorry, but I really do need to go to this show. Why won't you let me in, Bart?"

He released a big breath. "Horizon put you on a Do Not Admit list."

Trina laughed. "Oh, good gravy! How did he even know I was coming?" Then she shuddered. She glanced toward the dragon. Suddenly Trina felt creeped out, watched, as if he had been following her.

"He doesn't know you're here, babe. He put you on this list for all of his performances, at all venues, about five years ago. You've been banned from all Horizon Line concerts forever." Bartleby laughed. "He's probably so annoyed it's taken you this long to realize you've been blacklisted." He looked at her meaningfully. "So you will not be coming to the show tonight, Ms. Goldberg-Oneka. You'll be having dinner with me, at eight P.M. at this cute place in Little Tibet. Okay? Because The Go-Go can't give anyone with your name a ticket to this event. You understand?" He winked at her. Cautiously, she smiled. Bart knew she was going to the show.

"Thanks, man," she said. "I really appreciate it."

He gave her a big hug. "So good to see you, girl. It's been way too long." He sniffed. "And go take a shower, you stink!"

14.

She had a couple of hours to kill before the performance, so Trina took herself to lunch at a ridiculous café called My Attitude Is Gratitude in the textile district. She sat down at the long communal table and tried to look as unapproachable as possible.

The waitress came around and took everyone's pulses. She asked the man to Trina's right about his sleep quality and inquired if the woman sitting across from her had been making regular bowel movements. Trina normally hated these kinds of places, but she didn't have time to be picky. No menus, no choices, just a lot of personal questions from a wannabe shaman— but the food was always really good. Their meals came out a little while later. The woman was given a bitter green salad, barbecue tofu with sticky rice, and a bowl of sour fish broth for sipping. She leaned back from the table and said "Ah!" before digging in. The man's meal was a large collection of little dishes: fermented soybeans, herring poached in green tea, slow-cooked dark seaweed, various salty pickles, and vegetable fried rice. He peered down at his meal and said "Huh?" before eating eagerly and methodically. Trina enjoyed her steaming bowl of thick kudzu stew very much, just as she'd known she would.

"Do you like your meal?" asked the woman across from Trina.

"Yes," said Trina. "Very much. Although I'm always secretly hoping I won't."

The woman laughed. "I know exactly what you mean." She took a big bite of tofu and considered what Trina had just said. "I do miss the old days, sometimes.

My mother's meatloaf. Canned corn. I wake up with the weirdest cravings. Saltines. A warm Coke." She shook her head. "That's the thing The Seep never understood about us." She smiled. "That we sometimes like things even though they're bad for us."

Trina glanced at the man eating next to her. He appeared engrossed in his food, trying bites of the little dishes in different combinations. "Perhaps we should start a restaurant," said Trina. "One that serves only food that's bad for you, that will make you feel like shit."

The woman laughed again, revealing slightly bucked teeth and a gummy smile. Trina dug it. "Bad Attitude Café? Or Café Attitude?"

"Oh, I like that. Hey," said Trina softly. "What other things do you miss? About the old days?"

"More than I imagined I would, originally." She hesitated. "I miss making mistakes. I miss feeling lost and alone." She looked right at Trina, her eyes gleaming with something like hunger. "Isn't that strange?"

Trina turned away. "I can't say I know what you mean."

The waitress came back to their table with dessert. The man was given a small slice of chocolate avocado mousse cake, which he attacked, and some decaffeinated coffee made from herbs. Trina was served a little ramekin of pudding—a blend of coconut cream, sticky dates, and cardamom. The woman was given a piece of dark chocolate topped with chopped nuts and candied orange peel, along with mint tea. As she held a piece of chocolate in her mouth and swallowed the hot tea, she leaned back from the table and put a hand over her heart. Trina found the gesture inexplicably moving. She wanted to keep talking to this woman, but she didn't know what to say.

"Ask yourselves and each other, what would you truly love to experience at this moment?" the waitress asked. "How are you using the gift of your physical bodies? What will you do with your precious life?" She put a hand on Trina's shoulder and proceeded to knead the tension out of her neck. "And you, my dear, need to interrogate your substance use. I'm prescribing supplements to support your liver, but you must stop drinking so much."

Trina shrugged her hands away. "Okay, we're good!

CHANA PORTER

Thank you." She did take the supplements, however, accepting the bottle with a curt nod. The waitress bowed low and moved on to another table.

"So." The woman lifted an eyebrow at Trina and smiled. "How should we use the gift of our physical bodies?"

Trina hesitated. "Oh," she said. "Um, well . . ." She hadn't been touched by another person since Deeba's death. Could she now? The idea of another person taking her clothes off made her skin crawl. No, she couldn't do it. Trina opened her mouth to politely decline, but then she felt a hand on her thigh. When she remained silent, the hand stayed put, a warm, firm touch.

Heat pooled between Trina's legs. Her body called out for attention, touch, comfort, sensation. She wanted the woman to move her hand higher. Trina looked into the woman's warm, pleasing face, desire surging through her, both familiar and foreign. She could do this. She could lie down with another person. Afterward, maybe they could talk some more.

Cautiously, Trina leaned over and kissed her softly on the lips. The woman's hand was still on Trina's thigh. "Let's get out of here," Trina whispered, into a stranger's mouth.

THEY WENT TO a love motel two streets away. The woman swiped her credit stick in the door's slot and the light flashed green. She sat down on the perfectly round bed and smiled again. Trina hadn't even gotten her name.

"Uh," said Trina, pulling out her flask. "Want a drink?"

The woman shook her head and opened her arms. "Come here," she said.

Trina put the flask down. She leaned down and ruefully sniffed at her own armpit. Bart had been right—she did smell like old beer.

"Hey," Trina said. "I'm going to hop in the shower. Been on the road."

The woman winked invitingly. "You want company?"

She sniffed her armpit again and shook her head with a coy smile, faking a confidence she didn't feel. *Well, babe, fake it till you make it*. "Nah," she said. "I'll be quick." Trina locked herself in the little bathroom.

It was an entirely empty white box. Oh, dammit. She hadn't realized she was in a building made in Seep architecture. Why was taking a regular shower so difficult? She leaned her head against the wall.

"I want a normal shower," she mumbled. "No weird colored water or anything, just plain water, hot but not scalding, and some soap, please." A very serviceable, ordinary-looking shower grew from the wall. Trina didn't have to turn it on; it was already spraying water. She dropped her clothes onto the floor, which dipped, a depression forming around the small pile. The hole began to suds and foam with soapy water, agitating the dirty clothes. Trina groaned. "I didn't ask you to do that!" Well, her clothes *were* in need of a wash. And they'd be dry soon enough.

The woman's voice called in from beyond the door. "Everything okay in there?"

"Fine, fine." Trina got under the stream. The water felt so good, its temperature perfect. She ran her hands over her body. Her strong, long legs; her thin, pert butt; the rangy muscles of her arms and abs. She was an old wolf, but she still had it. Trina ran her hands along her long, dark hair. Back when they'd been young pups, people thought she and Horizon might be related, mostly because of their hair. Now hers was shot through with gray, while his was black as ever. She shivered and washed her face, which was lined with wrinkles, mostly laugh lines around her eyes from all those years with Deeba. The deep creases around her mouth had appeared in the last five years. Her haggard, wobbly throat. The warm water felt so good, she wanted to stay in it forever. She lightly cupped the palm of her hand over her groin. Could she really let another person touch her there?

TRINA TURNED OFF the water, then dried herself with long, slow strokes of the fluffy white towel. She looked at her clothes. They were now being dried in their little pit, hot air pushing and turning the laundry in short jerks. She took a deep breath and exited the bathroom wearing only a towel around her chest. The woman was already in bed, in her underwear and a tank top. Despite the warmth from the shower, Trina's hands and feet felt cold again, almost numb. She sat on the bed.

"You're all clean," said the woman. She slid a hand up Trina's leg and leaned in close. Trina sat motionless. If she could get the woman to talk more somehow, if she could figure out something to say herself, maybe she would relax. She had felt so warm at the restaurant, their conversation had flowed so easily.

"Tell me more things you miss about the old days," said Trina.

The woman started rubbing Trina's arms, her thighs. The sensations felt vaguely nice, but her mind felt disconnected from her body, as if the caresses were happening to someone else. "I don't miss STI screenings, I'll tell you that," the woman said, leaning in to kiss her. Her lips were warm and dry. A tongue snaked into Trina's mouth. "Why," she murmured. "What do you miss?"

That tightness returned at the back of Trina's throat, choking her with the thick, hard feeling of displacement, of being in the wrong place with the wrong person. *I miss my wife.* She stumbled to her feet.

"I'm really sorry," Trina said, grabbing her bag. She ducked into the bathroom and yanked her almost-but-not-quite-dry clothes out from the hole in the floor. "It's not you—I'm sorry!"

Still wearing the towel, Trina ran out the door onto the quiet street. She pulled on her clothes in the alley. No one blinked at her nudity or her subsequent dressing. Everyone just minded their own business. Trina shook her head. If she saw someone run out of a love motel and then get dressed in the street, she would ask if they needed help. But Trina was just old-fashioned that way. On impulse, she took out the pamphlet and held it to her chest. The thick, slick paper grew warm against her skin, as if it were hugging her.

Those who die but do not perish
continue to live
I wanna disappear I wanna disappear
oh yeah oh yeah

PART THREE
YOU CAN (NEVER) GO HOME AGAIN

15.

Trina stood outside The Go-Go and popped a piece of gum into her mouth. Only six pieces left.

She waited at the end of the long entry line. She wondered what she might say to Horizon, but knew these imaginary conversations rarely helped when it came time for an actual confrontation. If she had learned one thing in her fifty years, it was that life never gave you what you expected, for better or worse.

The doors opened and the line started to move. When Trina got to the front, the dragon at the door just waved her inside with a bored, taloned hand. It gave her a little wriggle of pleasure to think of Horizon trying to block her from attending his show and there being no actual system in place to do so.

She tapped out a message to Bartleby on her personal Electric Spirit console to say that she hoped their paths crossed again soon, xoxo. Trina hated the personal console, how it made everyone expect her to be always available, but sometimes it did come in handy. Deeba had made her get one because Trina liked taking long walks in the mountains by herself and one time (just once!), she'd accidentally Seeped so deeply with a redwood tree that she'd lost two days. She'd woken up half-starved and covered in dirt. Deeba had been beyond herself with grief. Maybe when Trina got back to the city, she'd throw the console into the goddamn ocean so it could Seep with the fishes. She got suddenly teary, then hated herself for her predictable emotions. Just earlier that day, she had debated between staying in Detroit and going to a cave in Peru or some other lofty fantasy of stepping into another life with ease. Who was she kidding? She had no life. No love to keep her tethered to a form or place. All her old friends had moved on, in some way or another—new careers, new communities, new forms—except old Bartleby. Maybe she should change her form, too, become a bird or a dolphin or a goddamn baby with no responsibilities. Give up on this life altogether and roll the dice on her next one. But Trina had labored for this body! She'd fought and kicked and clawed to have her insides match her outsides, and now people changed their faces as easily as getting a haircut. Trina knew then that she wouldn't change form, wouldn't go live in a cave in Peru. She just wanted to go back in time and live in those early, heady Seep years when she hadn't been afraid of anything.

Trina ordered a beer from the bar. Then the lights dimmed and the crowd hushed. The first act came on: a short black woman with pink hair, carrying some kind of long rubber mallet. She knelt on the stage in front of a hundred metal tubes of different lengths and sizes. The musician tapped and blew air, water, and bubbles through the tubes, producing different tones.

The sounds blended together, the music light, then dense, complex yet playful. Trina finished her beer and got another.

A blonde girl started twirling slowly on the dance floor, her body illuminated in a patina of blue and green. "Pretty," she said. "Pretty, pretty, pretty bird." Then she lay on the floor, spread out like a starfish. The audience was Seeping hard.

On a low, round sofa, a gaggle of club kids were passing around an unmarked brown bottle containing God knows what. They looked about seventeen years old, all tarted up in glitter and feathers like a pride of peacocks, their eyes already surging with the blue-green of The Seep. "Hey," she said, motioning to their bottle. "Is that such a good idea? Do you all even know what it is?"

A red-haired guy clapped a heavy hand on her shoulder. "Stop trying to control other people's experiences, lady."

Trina straightened up to her full height. "You need to take your hand off me right now."

The man scowled, taking in her outfit with particular distaste. "You're at a Horizon Line concert, not a church service." He walked away. Trina felt surprisingly stung by the disdain in his voice, the look in his eye. *The Compound called—they want their outfit back.*

The musician played on. Her melodies were never resolved, they just kept multiplying and building on each other as she looped a live recording underneath it all, capturing and weaving disparate melodies into a dense aural fabric. The blonde girl was still rolling on the ground, stroking the floorboards. Then she started coughing, jerking on the floor, unable to sit up.

Trina knelt beside her. "You want help?"

The woman nodded. Trina got her slowly to her feet and sat her down next to the four pretty boys on the couch. The bottle lay empty on the floor in front of them. They were all really dosed now. The five club kids sat together, their bodies soft and limp, heads pointing down to the floor, their costumes loose and ridiculous. They looked more like tired children than partygoers, but at least for now they were safe. Trina drank more of her beer.

All the club kids' heads snapped upright at the same

moment. They spoke in unison from the couch, as if they were a single being. "We're always safe and we're always together, Trina FastHorse Goldberg-Oneka."

Trina kept her voice calm, her breathing regular. The Seep responded to big emotional shifts, sometimes hurting when it was trying to help. "Hello," said Trina. "With whom am I speaking?"

"It's too late now, you know. What's done is done. This is the only way around the sun."

"Pardon me?" asked Trina. "Can you be more specific?"

Five sets of eyes bored into her. "We are made greater than the sum of our parts."

"Ah. So you're a new being, made from these different people?"

They bobbed their heads in affirmation. "Separation is wrong. It makes everyone sad."

"Hmm, perhaps," she said lightly. "But I'm not sure you got consent for this unification, did you?"

All heads tilted up like a haughty child's. "The little mind doesn't always know what it wants. But the Big Mind always knows."

"That's not fair. Freedom is important to us,

remember? We need to be free to make our own decisions, even when they make us sad."

"You are sad, Trina FastHorse Goldberg-Oneka, because you are alone. We don't want you to feel sad ever again. We love you so much, much more than you will ever know."

Trina started backing slowly away, putting more space between herself and the bodies. Something was really fucked-up here. Even if they'd all drunk a very strong distillation of The Seep, it shouldn't be affecting them like this. "Well," she said carefully. "You know that we humans love our free will. So let me be sad if I want to be sad. And give these people back their independent identities. They want to be separate, not together." Onstage, the woman with the pink hair worked frenetically toward a stunning crescendo.

They shook their heads no in one jerky movement. "Allowing people to make the Compound was wrong. It created sadness, not happiness. We will remedy this mistake by keeping everyone together." All five sets of eyes narrowed at Trina as the woman finished her piece in a series of loud banging gestures. She smiled and bowed at the audience, her lovely face dewy with sweat. "Sometimes people are very certain about what will make them happy, and they're wrong! The little mind doesn't know what it wants. You are sad, Trina, because you won't move on. You must join us and not be alone."

The crowd burst into an enthusiastic applause punctuated with whistles and cheers. The club kids opened their mouths very wide. They no longer appeared to have teeth or tongues, just a series of gaping black holes expanding outward.

"Stay there and don't come near me," said Trina softly. "I do not consent to this." From one of their hole-mouths, an old song Trina used to love began to play. It was a song she'd danced to with Deeba one New Year's Eve the winter they had first fallen in love.

She felt tears come to her eyes. What good was her life at the moment, anyway? Maybe they had a point.

She shuddered. "I don't appreciate this," she said. "You're hurting me."

Slowly, the five bodies began to rise, their movement perfectly synchronized. "You are wrong, Trina Oneka. We are not making you sad. We are revealing the sadness you carry around you like a coat, like a skin. Let us in, let us in, let us in . . ."

But their music and voices were drowned out by a louder sound. The room went dark, then flashes of light burst onstage in bright, swift patterns. The club-goers who were still sober enough to stand lurched to their feet, like a court receiving its queen. Horizon Line came out, joined by his band. Trina grabbed the gun in her bag and shoved it into her jacket pocket. The feeling of the cold, heavy metal made her feel safe, in control. The show had begun.

A chorus of ethereal voices sang out:

> *I wanna disappear*
> *I wanna disappear*
> *I wanna disappear*
> *oh yeah oh yeah oh yeah oh yeah*

Awash in the blue-green light, Horizon stood center stage dressed in gold and white, his long black hair draped down around him like a cape. Unsurprisingly, he looked beautiful. Here he was, in all his glory, the sun shining out over the horizon. The bodies imbued with Seep no longer paid any attention to Trina. She couldn't decide if she was grateful for this, as they were now swiftly moving toward the stage, a wave being drawn to shore. Horizon sang into a floating microphone:

> *Oh yeah, oh yeah, oh yeah*
> *Let me teach you how to disappear*
> *Let me teach you how to disappear*
> *Let me teach you how*
> *Let me teach you how*

The music came at her, snakelike and pulsing, rearing up in a surge of intensity. Trina felt it vibrate inside her, in her throat, her chest, buzzing between her ears. She hadn't experienced such a visceral reaction to a performance in a long time. Unless she'd been high on The Seep, of course.

Trina looked up. In the haze of the lights, little particles of bluish green floated like dust motes revealed by the sun. *Goddammit fucking shit*, she thought. This must have been what Bartleby had been warning her about. Horizon Line was dosing his audience, all for the sake of a light show. Was this part of his "Seep Alchemist" schtick? Red-bearded guy spun like a dervish, arms outstretched, head thrown back and mouth open, catching particles on his tongue. Trina turned and saw the dragon making out with a woman on a low divan. No one here was in the right mind to help. She grabbed her medicine bag and pulled on a mask, a hat with a brim, and a set of plant-based biodegradable gloves. She wasn't perfectly sealed off, but this would help. Then she took out a bottle of diluted charcoal water and chugged it down, hoping it would do something to neutralize The Seep she'd ingested so far.

Trina pushed her way through the crowd to the stage. Horizon Line was using his Seep wand to create a flock of clock birds. They fluttered around the stage to the rhythm of the music. The birds seemed terrified. The crowd, delighted, watched them flit to and fro. Horizon Line sang into the floating microphone:

> *Original numbers dissolve and form*
> *into Something Greater than themselves*

those who die but do not perish
continue to live
Let me teach you how to disappear!
We are The Shift
We are The Shift
We are The Shift

A figure drifted onstage, silhouetted by a cone of fire. Despite the panic she felt, Trina snorted at the cheesy stage magic. The fact that the world had ended didn't mean people had gotten better taste, that was for sure. The figure moved its head like a bird, staring out into the crowd. Its throat was piled high with necklaces of black and gray flowers, its body sheathed in a diaphanous black gown. Trina squinted through the Seep haze, the flashing lights. It was the boy from the Compound, dressed up as a lovely and terrifying dark bird.

Horizon Line laughed. "Here is my newest creation, Nevermore! A beautiful raven boy who's never Seeped before. Who wants to see his first Seep experience?"

In response, the crowd shouted and stomped their feet. Horizon Line helped the boy down from his floating platform. He tripped a little on his long black dress, but the crowd didn't seem to mind. Horizon Line, holding a small urn in his hands, gestured for the boy to kneel. The boy opened his mouth like a baby bird. Horizon Line poured a viscous, silvery liquid into his mouth, then bent low to kiss him deeply. The crowd went wild.

Trina took out her pamphlet. She tried to shield it from the falling Seep particles, but her efforts were of no use. "Pam?" she asked. "Why are you doing this? The Seep is supposed to value our free will! And our consent! You're doing great harm."

The pamphlet was hot now, and slick, almost too warm to hold. It had turned transparent and iridescent, like a dragonfly's wing. "Pam? Talk to me!"

The little voice manifested as hot breath in her ear. Trina listened closer and was surprised to find it was not one voice, but what sounded like dozens of quiet voices speaking in unison. *"We don't know what is happening. We are not all We, We are not unified as We have been since there was Time."* The voices grew even fainter. *"It's almost as if . . ."*

"What?" cried Trina. "As if what?" A person to her

left gave her a funny look. To be fair, it did look like she was fighting with herself.

The little chorus of voices spoke slowly, grappling with the words. *"As if Horizon has harnessed a little bit of The Seep for his own purposes."* The little voices grew dreamy. *"Who are we, now that we are not ourselves? Who are we, if we are not the sum of all of our parts?"* The voices seemed to almost shrug. *"It's interesting, to say the least. We can't wait to see what will happen next!"*

"Well I'm glad *you're* having a good time," said Trina. "'Cause it's freaking me out."

The little voices rose together in a shriek. *"We're freaked out, too, Trina! That's what's so interesting!"*

Trina walked through the crowd, asking people if they wanted to be lifted from the floor, if they wanted to get some fresh air, offering bottles of charcoal water. She even dragged one very fucked-up young person away from the downpour of Seep particles from the ceiling, covering their passed-out body with a coat on a couch. She held on to her medical kit in case anyone got really hurt. She took a deep breath and wiped her brow. They'd get through this.

And it felt good to be a doctor again, to be helpful, necessary.

"You're enjoying this," whispered the little voices.

Trina shrugged. "So?"

"Why do you feel like you need to have a job in order to be part of this world?"

Trina sighed. "You know what, Pam? No more talking, okay? Give it a rest."

"You don't need a function in order to be here, Trina. You are allowed to be, just as you are."

Trina balled up the pamphlet and shoved it deep into her jacket. "You know what, Pam? I'm telling, not asking you to shut up. We need to focus on the problem at hand, not analyze my emotional state. So be quiet!"

THE SENSATION OF hot breath in her ear disappeared. Trina watched a piece of The Seep waft down from the ceiling and melt into an exposed bit of her skin. Suddenly, the floor seemed to tilt and sway. Time stuttered, then lengthened out. Trina floated, adrift in a swirl of thoughts. She thought back to the war paradigm of the old days. How everyone thought they'd always live on a planet with war. *Things are better now*, she thought fiercely as tears welled in her eyes. *Things are better, even though I'm so fucking broken*. It had been about five years since Deeba had decided to become young again. She was now a happy little girl, living with a loving Persian couple in the South of France. She was growing up speaking Farsi, Arabic, French, and English, just like she'd wanted. And Trina had let her whole life go to rot, punishing her beloved home and her own body over Deeba's betrayal. Deeba had a new family, someone to kiss away her tears whenever she scraped her knee or didn't get along with someone in school. Trina couldn't even bring herself to find comfort in a nameless stranger in some love motel. Where Deeba was dynamic, Trina was stagnant. Where Deeba was young, Trina was old. Where Deeba was the future, Trina was mired in the past. Deeba was full of life, and Trina was courting death.

ON THE STAGE, a dozen bodies encircled the unmoving boy. He didn't even appear to be looking at anything, he was so lost in The Seep. Horizon Line ran around the stage, manic and cackling. This wasn't performance art, this was chaos. It wasn't freedom, it was violence. But maybe everyone else was right and she was wrong, Trina thought, her center lost and floating. She was a prude, a hack, stuck in her old life, unable to move on. But no longer. She touched the gun. Her destroyer of worlds. She bobbed her head in time to Horizon's catchy song. He was right. It was time to disappear.

16.

Trina didn't realize that she, too, had climbed onto the stage. She looked down and saw the gun in her hands.

Horizon Line stared at her, an odd smile on his lovely face. "Old friend," he said. "You came!"

"I came."

"I'm sorry I put you on the Do Not Admit list." He flashed her a wide grin. "They aren't very good at keeping people out, anyway." He spoke as if they were the only two people in the room. "I've thought of you so much lately!" Trina turned around, looking for the boy from the Compound, but she didn't see him. The audience had now merged with the stage, bodies writhing everywhere in dense clusters of movement. There was no longer a line between audience and performer. Whatever this experience was, they were all in it together now, including Trina, whether she liked it or not.

A clock bird whizzed by Trina's nose. She jerked back, startled, then lifted the gun. The pamphlet surged with heat in her other hand. The crowd swirled and shouted. Horizon Line stood calmly in front of her.

"Horizon," yelled Trina. "You can't use other people for your own purposes any longer. This stops now!"

He just kept on smiling, as if patiently waiting for the punchline to a joke. Trina pointed the gun at his chest, then pulled the trigger. It felt heavy and light at the same time, like a great bird taking flight.

In a single moment, all went quiet. Horizon Line and Trina sat together on a bench in a little garden.

"Thank you," Horizon Line said. "That's so much better." He looked up into the sky. The moon was full and bright. "I fear I've lost my taste for crowds."

Trina looked down at her hands. The gun was gone. She flexed her fingers, opened and closed her palms, then looked around the garden. She knew this place, but couldn't remember how or why. Next to the bench stood a little stone sculpture of an angel covering its face. She had definitely been here before, but when?

"I keep thinking about our last conversation," said Horizon Line. "And as you probably realize, the conversations we can't let go of have great things to teach us."

Trina craned her neck to look toward a house. The lights were on. There were sounds of a dinner party inside—laughing, voices talking, music playing low. Now she remembered this night.

"I wanted to tell you, Trina, that I finally understand what you were talking about. I was so mad at you, you know," continued Horizon. "I was so offended that you would use that word on me. It felt violent, like you were harming me. But what you were really saying was that I was harming you." He stared up at the full moon. "I've done a lot of wrong things in my life."

Trina looked back at the window. There, in the lamplight, she could see Deeba's shaved head. She longed to go inside, to take her into her arms once again, to feel her perfect density. But Trina didn't move. She remained with Horizon Line in the garden, because that was what she had done all those years ago.

"I misunderstood so many things," Horizon continued. "We can't just choose to erase or ignore the past. We're creating the future with everything from the past, at all times. We are all from the same Source, but our experiences have made us different, and that difference needs to be celebrated and remembered. You were right, Trina. Identity cannot be stepped into like pants or a pair of socks." As he spoke, his features began to change. The long nose disappeared, replaced by one that was short and round. His full lips grew meager, his chin weaker. His long, black hair receded until it disappeared. There was only a ring of gray around his spotted, bald head. Horizon

Line was now a very old white man. Trina's legs and arms buzzed with energy. The connection between her body and consciousness felt porous, as if she could float away from her physical being, from this garden of memory, from the past and even the future, if she wished. She was too uncertain to even feel fear. Trina held still, watching, morbidly curious for what was to come, like a portent of her own death.

He grasped Trina's hands in the moonlight. "I'm so glad to see you again, old friend, before I travel beyond all this. I'm sorry I hurt you on my journey. Forgive me?" He patted her hand vaguely, like a grandfather, and stood up. He groaned. "Oh! To feel the real weight of all these years!" He smiled at her, blissful as a baby. "How good it will feel to no longer live in the flesh." He looked up at the moon. He still smiled, even as his features began to fade away. The little nose, the thin mouth, the long ears, his whole face gone, as if rubbed off by a giant eraser. Then his skin dissolved, displaying tracks of muscle and bone, blood and entrails gleaming in the moonlight until they evaporated, too, like so much morning fog, until Horizon Line was nothing but a clacking skeleton, smiling at the moon. The skull turned to look at Trina from its eyeless sockets, holding up a set of hand bones in a gesture of goodbye. And then the skeleton too disappeared, shrouded and swirling in a fine glimmering golden mist that lifted up into the sky.

Trina turned back toward the house. She saw the garden door open, a head poking out from behind the doorjamb. It was Deeba, coming into the garden to see why Trina and Horizon Line had disappeared from the party for so long. She looked at her wife. And then Trina blinked in horror and astonishment, sadness and regret.

In the second her eyes closed and opened again, she was back onstage at The Go-Go. The loss of Deeba was fresh again, a raw wound at the center of her life. The crowd was naked now, piles of bodies rolling on the floor. It was pure movement, just limbs and cavities, openings, closings, a teeming mass of flesh trying to get closer to the Source. Their actions weren't specific enough to be sex, somehow more subtle and more gross than intercourse. If she didn't do something soon, they would all end up like

Horizon Line, ecstatically throwing off their flesh until they vibrated into light. And maybe that was what he had planned all along—to force everyone else into his own specific catharsis. Despite all his apologetic words, he had still worn that stolen face until right before the very end.

Just then, the fire alarm went off in a long, blinking wail. The sprinklers gushed on, the bodies on the floor jerking up in surprise. The whole party seemed to pause and look up, as if remembering themselves. For a moment, Trina thought this might be the elegant solution to her current problem, a deus ex machina of up-to-date fire codes. But then everyone went back to exactly what they had been doing before as water streamed down from the ceiling.

Trina walked through the piles of wet, writhing bodies. Arms reached up to caress her, to drag her down. She kicked them away. In the center of the stage, she saw the throng of bodies surrounding the boy from the Compound. He crouched smaller and smaller, his face twisted in pain, sinking into the floorboards. His gauzy black costume was ripped and dirty. Trina wiped the water and sweat from her face.

The sprinklers were soaking everything and everyone, and nothing was helping. *I don't know what to do*, she thought. But that was as fine a starting point as any.

"This is a door," she said, drawing an invisible line on the floor with her foot. Her words became a magic spell. She had decided it, and so it was. "It's a threshold between possibilities." She reached out to grab hold of the boy, pushing between the densely packed bodies. Finally, she seized his shoulder and did not let go.

Then she took out the engorged pamphlet, slick with Seep and pulsing with energy. Trina cried out with all her might, "Pam! Help me!"

The room fell away.

17.

When Trina opened her eyes, she was seated on a soundstage, her clothes and hair dry. The lights shined bright into her eyes while peppy talk-show music played from unseen speakers. Beyond the edge of the stage, a live studio audience clapped and cheered.

Next to her, a woman with puffy sleeves, bright bubblegum makeup, and big eighties hair spoke melodiously into a microphone. "Welcome, welcome,

welcome, to Soul Conversations! I'm so happy to be with you here today. I'm your host, The Seep!"

The studio audience cheered louder. Trina peered through the bright lights to make out their faces. She saw Deeba, sitting in the first row, wearing a pair of plaid pajamas and fuzzy orange slippers. Trina looked closer. There was another Deeba in a swimsuit, holding a beach umbrella. She squinted and saw that the whole audience was made up of different versions of Deeba: Deeba dressed for jury duty, Deeba in her purple-hair phase, Deeba ready for a ski trip wearing goggles, Deeba dusty with potting soil. Deeba on their wedding day in her bright green dress, holding sunflowers. Trina's eyes swam with tears.

"You may know me as the friendly neighborhood bodiless sentience that makes your life just a little bit easier. But I'm so much more than that!" The Seep beamed as the audience applauded. "I'm a lot of different things to a lot of different beings, but you can call me Pam." She smiled again. Her bright pink mouth was a wound, a cavity.

Trina cringed. Was this the same consciousness she had started feeling affection for? Embodied, it wasn't cute at all. Its approximation of humanity was alien, frightening. "Our guest today is Trina FastHorse Goldberg-Oneka, a relic from the Earth plane. She's stopped ingesting The Seep whenever possible and wears her old-fashioned clothes like a coat of armor. And when she finishes that last piece of gum, she's going to kill herself!"

The audience responded with a mix of cheers and boos. Trina turned to see a huge screen to her right, with her own image projected onto it. There was a chyron under her projected face that read:

TRINA DOESN'T WANT TO BE A PART OF
THE SEEP ANYMORE.

"Now, Ms. Goldberg-Oneka," said the smiling woman as she sat down next to Trina. "We understand you no longer want to be a part of The Seep. Will you tell us about that, dear?" She leaned back and took a sip of coffee from a bright pink mug that said THE SHTETL! BECAUSE YOU CAN NEVER GO HOME AGAIN.

"I never said that," said Trina slowly.

"But you think it," said the woman, her voice rising. "You feel that way all the time. You tried to kill Horizon Line, but you were really shooting at The Seep, at change, at everything he is and you're not. You hate us, Trina!"

The studio audience went "*Ooooooooh.*"

"I don't hate you," said Trina quietly. "But right now, I feel like you're breaking the deal you have with us. We're supposed to have free will. That includes being unhappy. That includes making the wrong decisions and getting hurt, or even doing something terrible. We're on this planet to grow and change, and sometimes that can only happen through struggle. Do you understand?"

The woman with the puffy sleeves started crying, huge fat tears streaking down from her eyes like blue-green algae. "But I'm trying so hard!" she cried. "All I want to do is make you happy. And you were so happy with me when I first arrived. Remember? Remember how happy we used to be? When I solved all the problems you wanted me to solve?"

Trina turned to see that the caption under her face had changed. It now read:

TRINA, DOCTOR/ARTIST, AGE 50, VERY

UNGRATEFUL

"And you're still unhappy! And you blame me! It's like you don't even remember everything I've done for you." The wet, blue-streaked face grew tight and pinched. "I love you and love you, I give and I give, and what do I get in return?"

Trina turned to the far side of the stage to see revelers from The Go-Go tangled together in a jumble of arms and legs. The boy from the Compound was in the middle of the club kids. They were pushing and pulling against him, as if trying to crawl inside him, to *be* him. Trina grimaced. If something didn't change, the boy and the mass would pull each other apart. All of this was caught in a feedback loop, together— Trina's hurt and anger at Deeba, her longing for relief and ecstasy, the desire of the partygoers to commune through excess, and the Compound boy's fear, all swirling with The Seep's intention to heal, to mend, to make everything better. The fighting and flailing bodies were now projected on the big screen. Their caption read:

IT WAS THE BEST OF TIMES, IT WAS THE WORST OF TIMES

"Well, The Seep," said Trina placidly, affecting a calm she didn't quite feel. "People need to give each other space to make choices. We can't live solely for other people. Even if it hurts them. Even when it breaks your heart."

The studio audience applauded. The jumbled family of arms and legs stopped fighting against one another for a moment. Trina looked out into the crowd. All of the Deebas disappeared except one, in the middle of the audience. She was wearing jeans and a flannel shirt, a Sunday outfit, clothes for just an ordinary day. Then, this Sunday middle-aged Deeba, plumper and wrinkled and more beautiful than ever, was standing next to Trina onstage. Trina reached out and touched the side of her face. Her skin was so soft, so familiar.

"I know you weren't trying to hurt me," said Trina. She tried to swallow the lump in her throat, but it didn't work. Blue-green started to drip down Deeba's face, starting at the very top of her head, the substance streaming down her eyes and cheeks. Trina resisted the urge to shut her eyes. Deeba's head began to shrink. Trina wanted to run away from the sight, but she was frozen in place. Her love shimmered and pulsed and grew smaller, her clothes billowing around her rapidly shrinking form. Deeba's eyes stared up at her, swirling with blue-green. Trina clutched her stomach, sickened by the change taking place. Deeba was becoming a baby. This was the vision she'd never wanted to see. This was why she hadn't gone to Deeba's transformation, even though Deeba had begged, pleaded with her to be at her side and hold her hand as she moved on.

"I won't go to your funeral," Trina had sobbed.

"Oh, babe," Deeba had said. "Go figure out who you are without me."

Now there was just a mound of clothes on the floor. At the center, something kicked and cried out. Trina knelt down. She moved Deeba's discarded shirt and saw a tiny baby wiggling on the ground, sticky with blue-green. Gently, she took the child into her arms and stood. She wiped the sticky stuff from her little eyes, her perfect nose, her sweet tiny mouth. Trina held Deeba to her chest, and a familiar feeling bloomed there.

"I hope," she said slowly, "that you are loved exactly the way you always wanted to be loved." *Because I love you, so so much*, she thought but didn't say. *And I always will.*

The child stared up at her. Did Deeba see her, know her? Did she understand her words? The child disappeared, and Trina found that she was holding herself. She took a deep shaky breath, her arms still wrapped in tight. She had been punishing herself for years, punishing herself for the loss of Deeba and how terrible she felt about that loss, a vicious circle sucking her under. No more. She would still feel sorrow, hurt, anger at that great gaping loss. But she wouldn't flagellate herself for those feelings. And eventually, eventually, those, too, would pass. She stood up a little straighter. Eventually, Trina would move on.

But The Seep stomped her feet and thrashed her arms like a child having a tantrum. "But you're still so sad! You're going to be sad for such a long time! Years and years and years—" Then her eyes grew wide. "Let me take it away," said The Seep. "Let me take the memories away, and you'll never know grief again." Her mouth rounded into a fierce black circle. The Seep spoke without moving her mouth. "I'll take it away, like I took away money and illness, the sickness of the land, the poison in the water and the air. I'll make it better, like I made the ice freeze again, the winters cold again, your cells healthy and whole again."

Trina felt a shiver run up her spine. She tried very hard to remain calm. She planted her feet, facing The Seep and its terrifying hole of a mouth. "But Pam," she said. "My memories are who I am. You take away my memories, you erase me. Existence is memory. Do you understand? You'd kill me. You'd murder Trina FastHorse Goldberg-Oneka, daughter of Rita and Samuel, a child of love. Trans woman. Artist. Doctor. Healer. Native American. Jew. You erase my memories, and you erase my lineage of ancestors—their pain, their triumphs, their passions, their dreams. No matter if the memories bring me pain. It's my pain! Let me have it."

The roiling mass of bodies spoke in unison. "If fear is the anticipation of loss, then grief is . . ."

HAPPY MEMORIES HAPPY MEMORIES
HAPPY MEMORIES HAPPY MEMORIES
HAPPY MEMORIES HAPPY MEMORIES
HAPPY MEMORIES HAPPY MEMORIES
HAPPY MEMORIES HAPPY MEMORIES
HAPPY MEMORIES HAPPY MEMORIES
HAPPY MEMORIES HAPPY MEMORIES
HAPPY MEMORIES HAPPY MEMORIES

A lifetime with Deeba spooled out. Cooking, sleeping, reading, laughing, fighting and making up, in apartments and houses, gardens and beaches and on mountain hikes. The memories fluttered away, becoming new memories of other lifetimes, of other people, other configurations of loving and love. A father, a son, a teacher, a student. The memories doubled and tripled over and over until they became just feeling and color, an impression of sensation. The image of light reflected over water. A profound, life-altering kiss. The voice of a loved one, ringing out like a bell.

THE BELL RINGS out, loud but low, taking all other sounds and sensations away in its wake. And then there is a moment of great blankness, a calm void of dark. In this creative dark, there exists only complete and utter possibility.

What do you wish to make?

The words are not seen—there is nothing to see— but they are felt, they are understood. We are inside the pamphlet now, but not the object. We are inside an idea. And that idea asks us again:

What do you wish to make?

TRINA FOUND HERSELF in a long hallway. She immediately recognized the light, unremarkable flooring, the smooth white walls. She was in the hospital, the same one she hadn't been to work at in many months. Yet she didn't know this particular hallway—it seemed impossibly long and narrow, as if it had been overstretched, then dotted with too many doors. All of the doors were closed and perfectly white, but some had big clean windows. Trina walked for a while down the hall, passing no one, seeing no signs of hospital life—no volunteers singing songs, no doctors, no healers or medicine men or priests. She stopped in front of a door with a window in it and peered through.

On the other side was her first apartment with Deeba. The ratty pullout couch sat proudly deflated in the center of the living room; Deeba's film books littered the coffee table: Jarman, Varda, Akerman. Trina's art supplies lay tucked tidily into a sunny corner where the light was best, next to the easel she had found on the street one lucky night. Trina blinked. She could almost hear the water boiling on the stove for a French press full of coffee. There was nothing for her here, not anymore.

She walked on.

The next door with a window was a view into The Shtetl. She saw Pina and YD behind the counter. YD winced as if in pain, Pina moved to steady her. YD's old body was breaking down. Trina touched the doorknob, to step into the scene, then stopped.

There were two more doors, side by side.

On the left was a moment from just a few days ago, outside Philz Coffee. The pretty boy looked earnestly at her and asked for directions away from kindness, to a place where he could be alone and uncountable, credit-free. Since that day, she had thought of a million things she might have said to him—a grand speech about grief, about not running away from your problems or trying to drown them out with other sensations. She'd tell him that to be human was to feel it all, throwing in a few clumsy but sincere analogies. But she didn't know him or his pain. He was her excuse to keep running from her own problems. She didn't even know his name.

On the right was a door back into the Horizon Line show. The kids were still tearing each other apart. She suspected that if she kept walking, she'd find more and more doors, an infinity of choices, in this hallway of her life. The Seep was like that. It would keep giving and giving and giving to Trina until she told it to stop.

Trina thought back to an old song from when she was a kid, a child's silly nothing they used to sing at summer camp. The song was about trying to move past a big tree, and came with accompanying hand motions.

> *If you can't go around it,*
> *can't go under it,*
> *can't go over it,*
> *you gotta go through it!*

She opened the door, humming.

TRINA WOKE UP on the lawn outside of The Go-Go. Kids in various stages of undress had been bundled up in blankets, shivering and huddled together, their mascara-streaked eyes examined by healers with little flashlights. It was very early in the morning. The dawn had a steamy quality, the morning light making the dew rise and hiss from the cool grasses. A lean, slightly hunched woman with lank blonde hair held a mug down to Trina. She accepted it, grateful to hold the warm ceramic between her hands.

"Drink up," said the woman. Her voice was familiar somehow. "You'll feel better."

"What is it?" Trina replied automatically.

"Hot water with lemon," the woman said with a smile, pushing her thick black plastic glasses up her nose. "Seep-free, of course."

Trina squinted up at her. "Bartleby?"

The woman sat down next to her but looked at the ground. "Hi, FastHorse."

"You're a woman now?" She looked around at the kids. The healers were taking them to the hospital in shifts. Horizon Line was nowhere to be seen. Trina closed her eyes and saw him again, a grinning skeleton vibrating into light. She shivered.

"I wanted to tell you, but part of me was afraid you wouldn't understand, or you wouldn't like it." She looked at Trina sideways. "Or that you'd be hurt, somehow?" Bartleby stretched her arms behind her back. "This is me, just plain old Bart. Just looking a different way, you know?" She bit her lip. "Or maybe you don't? I live like this about half the time. Feels better this way." Bart lightly touched Trina's hand, then drew it away. "But it's still me, your old friend." She smiled. "The one who doesn't like change."

Trina looked at the kind, owlish eyes behind thick glasses, the set of her jaw. The way she fiddled with her shirt sleeves when her hands weren't holding a book or a pen. This was Bartleby. And her masculine form—that was Bart, too. Trina still didn't get why anyone would want to live as two different forms. Seemed complicated, and well, time-consuming. She squeezed Bart's hand and held it. "I don't really understand, but that's okay. I'm happy for you, sweetie."

Bartleby nodded toward the boy from the Compound. "What's going to happen to him, you think?"

He was wrapped in a blanket, speaking excitedly to a group of healers and community members from The Go-Go. Trina couldn't make out what he was saying. One healer was writing down his words while another checked his pulse. A third person got him a cup of tea.

Trina shrugged. Her speech was still on her tongue, the one about grief and letting go. But as she watched the boy from afar, surrounded by good people who were listening and responding in real time, she knew it wasn't up to her to save him. If anything, in a twisted way of the miraculous, ridiculous world, he had saved her. She snorted. Maybe she should send him a thank-you card. A fruit basket. As for the speech she'd been practicing, about love and loss and all that jazz, well, the ride back to the city that used to be San Francisco was long enough. She could give it to herself, the one person who definitely needed to hear it. Anyway, Trina had things to attend to. It was time to go home.

She rose and brushed herself off. "Come and see me anytime, in any form," she said. "Don't be a stranger."

Bart blushed. "Will do."

They hugged, and Trina wandered off toward the train station, her medicine bag and leather jacket at her side. She suspected she would never see the gun or the gum again. Like so many of the things that she used to care about, they were lost for good. And that was fine.

18.

It was late in the afternoon when Trina walked into The Shtetl. Pina and YD stood behind the bar together, just like Trina's vision through the doorway— Pina holding YD as if to steady her, YD wincing in pain.

"Hey," Trina said. She opened her medicine bag on the bar counter and grabbed her Seep pen and an herbal muscle-relaxing salve of comfrey, turmeric,

devil's claw, and arnica. "I need you to tell me something straight, old girl."

"Well, hello to you, too." YD tried to smile but it
looked more like a grimace. "You don't call, you don't
write . . ."

"Yeah, yeah, yeah," continued Trina, waving her
hand as if to shoo her words away. She located a
bundle of seizing nerves near YD's upper spine and
got to work. The Seep spoke to her frozen shoulder,
whispering to relax, let go.

YD's face immediately softened.

Trina smiled. "Let me try that again. Hi, I missed
you. I love you." She winked at Pina. "Missed you too,
fur-face."

Pina frowned. "Her words seem nice, but she is not
being nice."

YD groaned in relief as Trina rubbed the salve
into her neck and shoulders. Pina reconsidered. "Or
maybe she is being nice, but her words are not so
nice? Hard to say."

Trina wiped down the Seep pen and replaced it into
her bag. Then she put her arms around YD. Under all
that herbal goo she smelled terrible—vaguely rotten

and sweet, like a moldy piece of fruit. "Okay, momma, I need you to be honest with me. Are you staying alive for my sake? Are you afraid that without you, something might happen to me?"

Great drops appeared in YD's cloudy eyes, but they did not fall. "You're so full of yourself," she said hoarsely. "Not everything in the world is about you, missy."

Trina's stomach growled loudly, and YD smiled, eager to be the one taking care rather than vice versa. "Pina, bring her a menu. Our Trina is hungry!"

Pina shuffled toward the kitchen. "You should listen to what she says, YD, she's finally making sense." Pina continued to grumble from the kitchen. "Normally, she says only stupid nonsense."

"Listen to me, YD." Trina met her gaze. "I know I've given you a hard time of it the last few years." She kissed her mottled cheek. "Sweetheart, if you're ready to go, go. I won't hold your life hostage." She nodded seriously. "And I'll survive. I promise."

YD squinted up at her. "What happened to you?"

Trina shrugged. "Existential quest. What happened to you?"

YD sighed. "I couldn't get out of bed for the last two days, couldn't sleep, couldn't eat, couldn't take a shit. My three favorite things." She nodded. "Ach, maybe it's finally time to go. I do want to see what death's colors look like."

Pina brought out a plate of blueberry blintzes with sour cream, a steaming cup of white cabbage soup, and a cup of black coffee. She slammed the dishes on the bar top with a little more force than usual.

"Pina!" said YD. "I told you to bring a menu!"

Pina shrugged. "You people," she said. "You don't know what you want." She grinned. "But I bring you what you need."

YD raised an eyebrow. "You're going to make an excellent restaurateur."

Trina didn't have a smart reply, for her mouth was full. She was very, very hungry.

Epilogue

YD had a lovely funeral. At The Shtetl, of course. She was handing the bar over to Pina and had spent the better part of the week cooking. It was how she wanted to show her love one last time.

They gathered on a Sunday in the late afternoon. The small restaurant was packed with longtime customers and friends, dancing, eating, drinking. They shared stories from YD's life and traded bites of food.

Magnificent cocktails of YD's design liberally poured forth, but Trina abstained. She had gone on a drinking bender, hadn't she, so why not try a sobriety bender? At least for a little while. Trina knew The Seep would leap to fix any cravings for her, if only she asked. It could make her feel perfectly sated after two drinks and never want more, or to dislike the taste of alcohol altogether, or to cease that old familiar feeling of warmth drinking gave her, rendering it rather useless.

But Trina didn't want any of these solutions. She wanted to sit in her struggle for a while longer. *Who knows*, she thought, accepting a hot glass of black tea served Russian-style, with a spoonful of Pina's homemade cherry jam. *Maybe I'll get into wine tasting when I'm three hundred years old.* A person wearing a tall, pointed red hat banged a spoon on their glass. Pina strode to the center of the room.

"I will sing a song for you to listen to now," Pina said. Her fur looked shiny in the candlelight. "I wrote it, but it is not mine. It is for you. After song, I will make a speech." Pina smiled, teeth glistening. "The speech is for my friend YD. I practiced it many times."

The room grew quiet. Pina stood tall, holding her

large paws still at her sides. She sang, in a strong, flat voice:

> There was a stream in a forest
> The forest was green and the stream was clear
> The rocks were black but some of them were gray
> Every thing is more than one color.
> Every thing is more than one shape.
> Look, a bird flies overhead!
> There is a song in everything.
> In all the grass and sand and skies
> There is a world in every world.
> A cub is rolling on her back.
> A cub is rolling on her back.
> A cub is rolling on her back.
> A cub is rolling on her back.

The crowd clapped and cheered, a small sea of glasses raised and waving. "YD," said Pina, turning to look at her. YD waved out from her small high couch like a queen. "Here is my speech for you. I have learned that humans call a group of bears a 'sloth' of bears. That is such a thing that humans would do, make up these silly names for groups of animals they don't even know. 'Sloth' is a way of calling someone lazy. But sloths are wonderful animals. They use their slowness to protect themselves. Before I came to The Shtetl, I was sad about the changes The Seep made in me. I could speak and think about life in a way that was not useful to me. I was no longer really a bear, but I was also not a human. I felt alone. I needed to move slowly in this new time. You gave me a home and a purpose. You never tried to change me. You gave me the protection of your slowness." Pina raised her glass. "We were sloth, together. And you are always my family, even when you are dead."

YD wiped her eyes. Pina banged her fist on the table with a hard smack. "Good good life! Good good death. To you. My friend."

The dessert was set to come out just after YD had died. She had joked several times about not having to wash any dishes after this party was over. As her eternal self left her body, she smiled brightly to all of her friends, her wrinkled face aglow, perhaps with recognition or perhaps only relief from pain. Trina watched her face closely, wondering if she could tell the progression of death's colors: white, reddish, and then perfect black. A priestess who had been conscripted by the hour caught her essence in a small glass jar and said the minimum blessings. YD had decided to pour her essence into the sea. The rebirth period typically took forty-nine days, but everyone knew to make room for the unexpected. No one knew quite what she'd become or where she would go, if she'd remember this life, the bar, her friends. The jar sparkled in the low light, a kaleidoscope of every color and no color. Trina felt the back of her throat tighten. She'd always known her friend was beautiful, but this was almost too much. *What a miracle we are*, Trina thought. Afterward, they ate YD's honey cake with small cups of strong coffee. Then it was time to go home.

Just because Trina couldn't resist pulling the scab off a healing wound, when she got back to her house, she put on the song that had played from The Seep's open mouth. It was the same song she and Deeba had danced to all those years ago, the winter they'd fallen in love—"Young Americans" by David Bowie. Finally, for the first time since Deeba had died, she really let the tears pour. She cried for the friends she had lost, her family, the streets that had lost their names. She cried for all those years she'd gotten older but not wiser. Finally, Trina cried for immortality. It was a cheap trick those aliens had played on us. Who would have thought that clear, certain death was not a curse to break, but a precious gift?

Deeba had been right, of course, just as she always had been. It was brave and beautiful to go back to the beginning. Trina wasn't ready yet. But she had plenty of time. The chorus kicked in. *All night* . . . Dead singer, immortal song. Trina wiped her eyes. The song ended, and another began. She got up to clean the living room.

After attending to the miles of crusty dishes, Trina sorted old newspapers and stacked up books to donate. She boxed up most of Deeba's things to give away, then looked around her living room. She could see the floor! What a nice change. But there was an emptiness present here now. Perhaps the house was too large for just one person.

Trina looked at Deeba's desk, still in the far corner

by the fireplace, facing a large window into the over-grown garden. The living room got spectacular light. She went into the hall closet and dragged out her tall, old wooden easel, the same one she had found on the street so many years ago, thrown out in the days of curbside garbage pickup. Trina remembered the joy she'd felt that night, dragging it up the five flights of stairs to her apartment. How the big easel moved with her each time she got a new place, until it was forgotten in a closet along with the rest of her art practice. What would it be like to make art without thinking of it as a career? To make something for no other reason than creation itself? Trina pulled the desk into the center of the room, next to the boxes marked GIVE AWAY. She opened the legs of the easel and stared at it in the context of her bare space. It looked good.

IN THE KITCHEN, Trina drank a glass of water and wiped her sweaty brow. There still was a lot of work left. But others were arriving later to help with the more serious jobs: the yard work, the sad fish pond, the moving and sorting of boxes. Pina was coming, happy to spend all day hauling sticks in the yard, along with that busybody Blane and his friendly otter, plus Mariam and Emma and Peaton. (Allie was in India, living in a cave. Trina didn't think she'd be coming back anytime soon.)

Trina opened her fridge. The cupboard was bare. Well, she still needed to feed people. She pressed her Electric Spirit console. *There's no shame in getting takeout*, she thought. *It's still a dinner party.*

Tips for Attending a Dinner Party
When Your World Has Ended
and
Another World Is Just Beginning

SAVOR EVERY LITTLE spoonful. Put your fork down between bites and actually listen to the conversation bubbling around you. Remember, you're here for the experience. At the end of your long, languorous evening, should your host refuse you once, even twice, persevere—wash as many dishes as you can! Relish the feeling of the warm water, the steam on your face, the easy certainty of a dirty bowl made clean again. There is always work to be done, so why not do it? Everything can suddenly be taken away, like we're just birds flying blissfully into a pane of glass. Enjoy the flavor of these intimate kitchen conversations. Ask more questions than you provide answers. When you do speak about yourself, don't rehash old party material. Be vulnerable! And remember, before you ask your host where to put things, make sure to look in the cabinets and drawers. She won't mind if her sugar bowl is put away in the wrong place when she wakes up to a kitchen she didn't have to clean. As for you, you will probably wake up tomorrow, too. The sun will probably rise. Breath will probably move in and out of your lungs, blood will probably pump despite your amazing broken heart. Right now, you have a body, a mind, and a memory that extends backward through time's infinite doorways. You are an everyday miracle. Enjoy life. Because even with the promise of forever, nothing lasts.

Acknowledgments

A great many people gave their energy and support to me in the years I spent writing this book, too many to name. Here are the highlights. My parents, Susan and Steven Porter, are incredible cheerleaders and wise friends. My mother, a former high school English teacher, made edits on manuscripts for years before I had an agent or editor. Sarah Bolling at The Gernert Company is the finest agent I could hope for, and without her vision this book would not be what it is today. Thank you, Tom Mayer, for introducing us. My wonderful editor Amara Hoshijo, rockstar publicist Monica White, Rachel Kowal, and the rest of the fine people at Soho Press gave me the debut I had been dreaming of for a long time. Biggest thanks possible to Rachel Pollack, Nicola Morris, and John McManus at Goddard College where I began writing *The Seep* as my MFA thesis, and to Paul Selig for helping me hear my own voice. I'm very lucky to have Levi Bentley as a reader of my work—our conversations over the years changed the shape of the narrative a great deal. My dear Eri Nox read early drafts with care (and printed them out for me at work, much to the chagrin of their boss.) To my dinner party witches: Katharine Duckett, Laura Lamb, Mariam Bazeed, Liz Gorinsky, Patricia Black, ray ferreira, Tyler Hoyt, James Dean Palmer, Myah Shein. Our care of each other made my utopia imaginable.

Meghan McNamara, cofounder of the Octavia Project—you make me a better person, and a deeper thinker. And our RPG group certainly influenced my headspace. Thank you for reading *The Seep* in the earliest incarnations and encouraging me to focus on Trina's journey. Thank you darling Perel, Josephine Stewart, Eric Powell Holm, for the early draft cheerleading and the caregiving. Thank you Sarah Einspanier for the final push pep talks and synchronicity. Austin Wulliman and Brad Balliet for deep reading.

Geoffrey Olsen, for walking down the road with me.

Ann and Jeff VanderMeer, for being my fairy godparents of the weird world of fiction writing.

The MacDowell Colony and Veltin Studio, where I picked myself up and rewrote yet again. The incredible artists of all disciplines I met there deeply influenced this process. Those conversations about the artist life continue to inspire my writing practice daily.

Thank you to dear ones who loved me through this long process: Dinah Grossman, Lauren Monroe, Cody Pherigo, Jess Joseph, Lecta Nadal, my dear brother Matt Porter.

And last but never least, Ted Hearne. For embracing my wild. My attitude is gratitude.